Goddess Girls

ELPIS
THE
HOPEFUL

READ ALL THE BOOKS IN THE GODDESS GIRLS SERIES!

Goddess Girls

ELPIS
THE
HOPEFUL

JOAN HOLUB & SUZANNE WILLIAMS

Aladdin

NEW YORK   LONDON   TORONTO   SYDNEY   NEW DELHI

ALADDIN

An imprint of Simon & Schuster Children's Publishing Division
1230 Avenue of the Americas, New York, New York 10020
First Aladdin hardcover edition December 2023
Text copyright © 2023 by Joan Holub and Suzanne Williams
Jacket illustrations copyright © 2023 by Alan Batson
Also available in an Aladdin paperback edition.
For information about special discounts for bulk purchases, please contact Simon & Schuster
Special Sales at 1-866-506-1949 or business@simonandschuster.com.
The Simon & Schuster Speakers Bureau can bring authors to your live event. For more
information or to book an event contact the Simon & Schuster Speakers Bureau
at 1-866-248-3049 or visit our website at www.simonspeakers.com.
Series designed by Karin Paprocki
Jacket designed by Alicia Mikles
Interior designed by Mike Rosamilia
The text of this book was set in Baskerville.
Manufactured in the United States of America 1023 OFF
2 4 6 8 10 9 7 5 3 1
Library of Congress Control Number 2023006311
ISBN 9781534457492 (hc)
ISBN 9781534457485 (pbk)
ISBN 9781534457508 (ebook)

We appreciate our mega-amazing readers!

For
Calypso & Persephone W.,
Damien S.,
Kristin H., Paul H., Julie H., Saad S.,
George H., Kate H.,
Barbara E., Andy S., Emily S.,
Bonnie G., Grant G., Grace G.,
Niki G., Neel G., Palmer G., and Townes G.

J.H & S.W.

CONTENTS

Goddess Girls

ELPIS
THE
HOPEFUL

Pronunciation Guide

How to say some of the names in this book:

Apate (ah•PAH•tee)

Amphitrite (am•fih•TRI•tee)

Aphrodite (af•roh•DI•tee)

Ares (EH•reez)

Artemis (AR•teh•miss)

Athena (uh•THEE•nuh)

Elpis (EL•piss)

Hades (HAY•deez)

Hera (HEH•ruh)

Koalemos (koh•AH•leh•mohs)

Lysander (lih•SAN•dur)

Moros (MO•rohs)

Pandora (pan•DOHR•uh)

Pericles (PEH•rih•kleez)

Persephone (per•SEF•oh•nee)

Pheme (FEE•mee)

Plato (PLAY•toh)

Poseidon (puh•SI•duhn)

Socrates (SOCK•ruh•teez)

Zelos (ZEE•los)

Zeus (ZOOS)

1

A Precious Day

"WHAT AN AMAZING DAY!" ELPIS SHOUTED up to the bright blue sky one Monday morning. Here on Mytikas, *every* day was perfect and precious, in her humble opinion. Mytikas was the highest peak on Mount Olympus, which was the tallest mountain in Greece. From atop it, she had a brilliant view of all the little towns, villages, forests, and lakes far below her.

Although Elpis could see, hear, and speak like

a human, she wasn't mortal. Or immortal, either. Nope! She was a *real . . . live . . .* bubble! The sparkly, golden bubble of "Hope," to be exact. Until a few months ago, she'd spent her life locked inside a dark box along with nine horrible, troublemaking bubbles. So being free amid all this beauty was awesome!

Her freedom was mostly a result of sneakiness on her part, though. It had come about after a Titan godboy named Epimetheus had brought that awful box to Mount Olympus Academy (MOA for short). There, the box had fallen into the hands of a curious student named Pandora, who'd discovered the secret to opening it!

While Elpis remained trapped in the box, those trouble bubbles escaped. They managed to bump into nine MOA students, temporarily changing each student's personality for the worse. Once Elpis escaped, she *gloop*ed the trouble bubbles out of those students, though, returning them to normal.

Then, while Pandora captured all the other bubbles, Elpis stealthily bobbled away to this peak. Ever since that crazy day, she'd worried she might be caught and returned to the box too. She really *hoped* that would never happen!

For now, Elpis shook off thoughts of the past. Leaving her perch, she hitched a ride on an air current. *Whee!* Like a kite or a bird, she was carried along by the current, gracefully gliding down, down, down the slope of Mount Olympus. How she *loved* floating along on this fresh mountain air!

She was always careful on such travels, though. The world was quite unsafe for someone like her.

Someone small and fragile. Like most bubbles, she was made of water, soap, and air, and she was only a few inches wide.

As far as she knew, only two beings had ever been able to see her. Pandora, of course. And Zeus, the most powerful Olympian ever! He was King of the Gods and Ruler of the Heavens, and the principal of Mount Olympus Academy, too. Therefore, Elpis stayed away from that place. Because Zeus might not like it if he discovered she roamed free.

Sure, she sometimes got lonely being all by herself. But a busy, helpful life spent alone was better than being trapped with those unfriendly trouble bubbles, who'd argued and plotted nonstop. As if troublemaking were an Olympic sport!

Such bad thoughts fell away as she swooped ever

lower, glorying in the day. Here on Mount Olympus's beautiful Mytikas, she couldn't help but be happy. And hopeful! Skirting the edge of a village, she was on the lookout for signs of *un*happiness right now, though. That was how she spent most of her time— offering hope to others in times of trouble.

The homes she spied below were built of wood and mud bricks, each with wooden shutters on the windows and a small courtyard or garden. Here on the mountainside, villagers were going about their day. But then . . .

Crack! Out of nowhere, a thunderbolt shot down from the sky. She gasped as it struck one of the homes. *Ka-boom!* Half of it was instantly wrecked! As Elpis watched in horror, a family of four rushed out of the house, seeking safety outdoors.

"Oh no! Our home! Half of it is gone!" wailed the mortal woman who'd fled the house. She held a crying baby in her arms.

"Destroyed!" wailed the kind-looking man beside her. "What'll we do?" He held the hand of his terrified little son, who clung to him.

Just then, a shadow passed overhead. Elpis glanced up in time to see a big, muscled guy with wild red hair and a beard zoom high across the sky. It was Zeus—riding away on his amazing white-winged horse, Pegasus! He must've thrown that thunderbolt! As the whole world knew, Zeus was famous for the huge, terrifying thunderbolts he wielded.

Anger filled her. How could he have been so careless? A family's home had been half ruined by that bolt. Her heart ached for them. Yet he didn't seem to care. Ignoring the damage he'd caused, he flew onward, never even slowing as he headed toward the Academy.

Well, *she* wouldn't ignore the misfortune he'd caused. Unlike Zeus, she would help them! (Her name was *Elp*is for a reason, she liked to think. Because she put the "elp" in the word "help"!)

Quickly, she drifted closer to the family. From a few feet away, she blew out four small bubbles, each the size of a dandelion puff. "Hope," she whispered, blowing the same word into each bubble. As fast as she created them, the hope-filled bubbles flew free of her and sailed toward that sad family.

Invisible to the people of the town, each of her bubbles bumped against the cheek of one of the four members of that family. *Pop! Pop! Pop! Pop!* As the bubbles popped, the family was filled with the magic of hope. Within seconds, their tears began to dry.

Now the father studied their broken house. "Well, at least half of it's still standing," he said, perking up a little.

"Yes! We can always rebuild," the mother added. "I'm just glad our family is safe."

"Me too," said the little boy, still hugging his dad's leg.

"Goo-goo," cooed the baby.

Elpis figured that was the baby's way of being hopeful too.

Having heard the crack of the thunderbolt and fearing some catastrophe, neighbors were now pouring outside to gather around the family. When they saw what had happened, they stepped in to help.

One man offered to bring the family wood planks. Another offered mud bricks. Still other villagers offered food, furniture, hammers, and nails. And many volunteered to spend time working to rebuild the house.

It pleased Elpis to see this nice family's hopes lifted even higher by their neighbors' kindnesses. However, this *never* should have happened. Zeus had been unforgivably careless.

Gazing up at the puffy clouds overhead, she saw that he and Pegasus had disappeared from view. Before she could think better of it, she issued a command. "Magic breeze, come to me, please!" No sooner had she uttered these words than a glittery breeze whooshed close, causing her to momentarily bob this way and that in the air.

Once she'd settled again, she told the breeze, "Please deliver this message to Zeus. Tell him that I, Elpis the Bubble, *hope* he will be more careful where he throws his bolts in the future. Because today one of them half destroyed a family's home." Feeling fresh anger at the memory of the incident, she added, "Shame on him!"

"I will deliver this message, as you wish," the breeze promised as it gently whirled and swirled around her.

No sooner had the breeze whipped away toward the Academy than Elpis began to worry that she'd made a terrible mistake. If she'd been face-to-face with Zeus, she'd never have dared to say such things to him. After all, Zeus was King of the Gods. She was just a *bubble*! So maybe her message was ill-advised? It could even land her in trouble!

"I hope he doesn't take it the wrong way and think I'm trying to boss him around," she murmured to herself.

Zeus was the one who had created her and the trouble bubbles in the first place. While *she* was golden and glittery, he'd colored the other bubbles blue, purple, green, orange, yellow, pink, red, turquoise, and chartreuse. He'd meant for the nine naughty bubbles to help him and the other Olympian goddesses and gods battle their Titan foes in a terrible war called the Titanomachy.

So it was no surprise that those bubbles were not good-hearted. They'd been created to cause mischief and thwart enemies! After the war, Zeus had boxed them up to keep the world safe. Her, too, which wasn't really fair, since she'd brought no trouble.

But if her message made him mad enough, might he *gloop* her back inside that box with those awful other bubbles for the rest of eternity?

Another hour passed as Elpis delivered hope here and there. To a farmer who hoped for healthy crops. To a child who hoped for a baby brother.

And then . . . whoosh! Out of nowhere, a new wind whipped up around her. It sent her loop-de-looping in the air.

"Stop! Stop! You'll make me pop!" she called to the wind.

When the pesky wind finally stopped blowing, she bobbed to a halt in midair, just inches from a firethorn bush. Carefully, she backed away. Many of these prickly bushes (also called pyracantha) grew in Greece. With their white flowers and red berries, they were pretty. But dangerous. To her, anyway. Bubbles did not fare well around sharp thorns!

"Message for Elpis from Zeus, King of the Gods and Ruler of the Heavens!" called the wind.

Uh-oh. Elpis groaned. "Already? That was fast."

"Art thou Elpis?" it guessed.

"Well . . . y-yes," she replied. This had to be about that note she'd sent. She was surprised Zeus would reply so quickly (or at all), but MOA wasn't that far away. And these message winds moved fast!

Argh! Zeus probably would never have noticed she was still on the loose but for that dumb message she'd sent in the heat of anger. Now she'd drawn his attention!

"Am I in t-trouble?" Elpis asked the wind.

"Zeus summons youuu to Mount Olympusss Academeee," it whoosh-spoke, ignoring her question.

Was this summons a good or a bad thing? If she *wasn't* in trouble, maybe Zeus just wanted to discuss what had happened to that family. Or ask her advice about what he could do to prevent future such mishaps. She kind of *would* like to speak with him. To caution him to be more careful with his bolts!

"I'm to give you a speedy ride to MOA," added the wind. "Let's go. Zeus doesn't like to be kept waiting!"

So saying, the magic wind abruptly whipped itself into a small tornado, one just big enough to carry her. Whirling gently, it wrapped itself around Elpis. Then, before she could protest, she was whisked away from the village.

2

The Academy

THE TINY TORNADO WHOOSHED WILDLY, BUT
all was calm at its center, where Elpis was nestled.
New hope sprang up in her as she was carried along
toward MOA. Because this could be her chance to
explain to Zeus the work she was doing! How the
hope she spread each day helped keep his sub-
jects from despairing over troubles big and small.

(Including troubles accidentally caused by the King of the Gods!)

In the short time the other nine bubbles had escaped their box, they'd released a *lot* of troubles into the world. Troubles that could never be reined back in. Not completely, anyway. Fighting the spread of the sadness and hopelessness those other bubbles had caused kept her super busy!

If Zeus could be convinced to value the work she did, he might decide to let her roam free forever. *Woo-hoo!* (On the other hand, if her message had only made him angry, he might not be in a mood to listen. *Boo-hiss!*)

Eventually, the small tornado transport unfurled enough that Elpis could view the Academy up ahead. She hadn't seen much of it the last time she was here. She'd been too busy de-troubling various MOA students from the mischief done to them by the other bubbles.

Now, though, she couldn't help but admire this majestic school for immortals (and a few lucky mortals and spirits). It gleamed in the sunlight atop Mount Olympus. Built of polished white stone, it was five stories tall and surrounded on all sides by dozens of Ionic columns. Low-relief statues called friezes were sculpted just below its peaked rooftop.

"The Academy is *so* beautiful!" Elpis exclaimed.

"Yessss," murmured the wind.

When they reached the massive bronze doors at the top of the Academy's front steps, she wondered how they'd enter. Luckily, just then the doors opened and some students spilled outside. The wind took advantage of this and whooshed her inside.

"Wow!" Elpis breathed, marveling anew at the grandeur she encountered. Marble tiles shone on MOA's floors, and the ceilings were covered with paintings illustrating the glorious exploits of the goddesses and gods. One scene showed Zeus battling spear-carrying Titan giants as they tried to storm Mount Olympus. Another showed him driving a chariot across the sky while hurling thunderbolts into the clouds.

The wind zoomed her down a hallway, high above the heads of teachers and students moving here and there below. Elpis watched a girl with long turquoise hair sip from one of the fancy fountains set along the walls. Afterward, the girl's skin sparkled more brightly as if powdered by golden glitter. This glitter indicated that she was an immortal goddessgirl, Elpis knew. Though similar sparkles covered Elpis, she *wasn't* immortal. Too bad, because if she were, she wouldn't have to constantly worry about getting popped!

"Amphitrite, where ya going?" another girl called, waving and rushing over to the turquoise-haired girl. This yellow-haired girl was Pandora! When Pandora drank from the fountain too, her skin didn't sparkle like Amphitrite's did. That was because Pandora was a mortal, one of the few who went to MOA.

Swept along on the breeze near the ceiling, Elpis remained invisible to students rushing back and forth below as they chatted or opened lockers. Eventually the wind hesitated at a turn in the hallway, seeming unsure which direction to take. As Elpis awaited its decision, her attention was caught by four girls gathered around a poster hanging alongside a classroom door labeled HERO-OLOGY. The poster read:

WINTER BALL IN THE HALL COMPETITION!
Our annual celebration of winter
will take place on December 1.
Submit art and design decoration ideas
to the front office by this Friday.

All four girls wore cute sandals and chitons—flowing gowns that were popular in Greece. A gold *GG* charm hung from a necklace each of them wore, and their skin sparkled and shimmered. Which meant they were goddessgirls. Yes! She recognized them from her last visit here—Athena, Persephone, Aphrodite, and Artemis. They were among those who had gotten bumped by trouble bubbles, causing them to act *very* unlike themselves.

Zeus's brainy brown-haired daughter, Athena, for example, had fallen under the spell of a "Ditz" bubble. As a result, she'd acted ditzy—as in *airheaded*— often staring blankly off into space instead of thinking smart thoughts or studying in her usual way. And the normally super-nice red-haired Persephone had become angry at everyone after getting bumped by an "Anger" bubble.

Elpis had helped rid those four girls of trouble bubbles. And she had done the same for four other students, and even Zeus himself! But she'd been invisible to these girls then, and no doubt was now as well.

As the wind continued to hesitate, still directionally confused, she listened in on the girls' conversation as they discussed school, homework, extracurriculars, and such. They sounded like . . . *friends*. What would it be like to have friends? Truly good ones—not troublemakers like those nine awful bubbles. She could only imagine.

After the girls walked off, a group of boys came along. Each wore a tunic—a plain, knee-length version of a girl's chiton. One boy carried a trident, which looked sort of like a pitchfork. She remembered him—the godboy Poseidon. She'd *gloop*ed a "Scaredy-cat" bubble out of him. Eyeing his sharp-tipped trident, she couldn't help but be glad the indecisive wind was keeping her high away from it!

A frowny boy in the group, with thick black-and-green hair that hung forward over one eye, paused to study the poster. Noting his interest, Poseidon nudged him, snickering. "Dude, you thinking of doing some art all of a sudden? You do realize you'd have to actually *talk to people* to participate in an event like that, right? And do you even know how to draw?"

Looking somewhat embarrassed at being caught out, the frowny boy shoved his black-and-green locks out of his face to glare at Poseidon. "Remember when I asked for your opinion? Yeah, me neither."

Poseidon's head jerked back in surprise. Taken aback by the boy's fierceness, he said, "Sorry. Whatever floats your boat, I guess."

The other boy relaxed instantly. Seeming to regret his sharp words, he elbowed Poseidon. "*Boat.* Ha! I get it," he said. "Because you're godboy of the sea."

"Yeah, duh," said Poseidon, all laughter again. With that, both boys turned away from the poster and rushed off to catch up with their friends.

Seconds later, the black-and-green-haired boy returned, however. After peering both ways as if to make sure no one was watching (he couldn't have known Elpis floated high above him), he stepped up to the poster. Quickly, he read all the information on it. Then he straightened and heaved a sigh. "If only . . . ," he mumbled to himself. Then he shook his head. "Nope. No point getting my hopes up." With a shrug, he ambled away.

Whoa, talk about negativity! Elpis wasn't sure exactly what the boy's hopes were, but they had something to do with that poster. She was about to send a helpful hope bubble to follow in his direction when . … whoosh! Having finally made a decision about which direction to go, the wind blew her down another hall.

A minute later, they zoomed from that hall, in through a doorway, and onward through an office past a lady with nine heads. *Whoosh!* On they went, passing through another bigger doorway and into a bigger office. There the wind abruptly stopped, leaving her suspended in midair.

Eek! Seated before Elpis was a powerful-looking guy with the biggest muscles she'd ever seen. Zeus!

3

Bubble Girl

Zzzz. ZEUS'S EYES WERE CLOSED. HE WAS SLEEP-
ing. And snoring too, while seated upon a huge
golden throne behind an equally huge desk. His
head was bent forward, with one bearded cheek rest-
ing on his forearms, which were folded on the desktop. Though a two-foot-long sandwich sat on a plate
nearby, only one bite had been taken from it. He was

a busy guy. Had his work here tired him out so much that he couldn't even finish his sandwich before falling asleep? It seemed so!

Zeus had summoned her here, and Elpis had come as requested. Should she wake him up? Or would startling him make him mad? Maybe she should just wait till he woke on his own?

"What do I do now?" she asked the wind that had brought her here. But she got no reply. Because that wind had already zipped away, she realized. *Argh!* She'd have to face Zeus alone!

"Well, thanks a lot," she mumbled, though the wind was likely too far away by now to hear her. Since she actually wished she could chicken out of this meeting herself, she *did* understand that wind making a speedy getaway!

While trying to decide what to do, she gazed around Zeus's office. It was messier than she would have expected the office of the King of the Gods to be. Everywhere she looked, there were piles of random junk. In front of his desk stood a row of chairs with scorch marks (from thunderbolts?) on their cushions. It looked to her like perhaps someone had cleaned up in here some time ago, but Zeus was slowly messing it up again.

Elpis floated herself over till she was level with Zeus's big head, yet still some distance away. As she bobbed in place, she studied him. She'd seen him earlier today riding Pegasus, of course. And she'd sort of met him, and some of the Mount Olympus Academy students, too. That was back when the trouble bubbles were on the loose and causing mayhem in these very halls. After helping Pandora to catch them, Elpis had happily heard nothing from Zeus.

Why, oh, why did I draw his attention to me today? she wondered again. It wasn't like Zeus had given her permission to roam loose. He'd simply never noticed that she hadn't been recaptured. When she'd disappeared, he'd been recovering from being bumped by a "Lazy" trouble bubble. One that had caused this powerful and (usually) energetic guy to temporarily become . . . well, *lazy*. Kind of like he looked now, snoozing away.

Maybe she should follow the wind's example and sneak out of here. Go back to her mountain peak and pretend she'd never gotten his summons. Maybe Zeus would forget all about her again? Quickly, she bobbed herself halfway back to the door.

But there she paused. "No," she whispered to herself. "I *won't* chicken out."

She needed to know what he wanted. And, well, she had some questions for *him*. Like why had he bolt-bombed that house in the village today?

Elpis headed for the big desk again, determined now to wake him. Slowing, she bobbed closer to him, avoiding his prickly beard as any smart bubble would. Then . . . ever so gently, so that she didn't accidentally pop herself . . . she bumped the tip of his nose. *Boop!*

She darted away from him again, waiting to see if he'd wake up. Nope. He snored on.

"Zeus," she hiss-whispered. No response. Elpis moved close again and bumped his nose harder. "ZEUS!" she yelled.

Well, *that* woke him up! Instantly, he jerked upright in his seat. One of his big, meaty hands shot out and knocked the plate with the sandwich halfway across his desktop. His other arm jerked outward too, sweeping papers, knickknacks, and a couple of trophies off the desk and onto the floor. *Crash!* He reared back in his throne, causing it to topple backward, taking him with it!

His muscled arms and big sandaled feet flew up in the air, flailing wildly. Then . . . BAM! The back of his throne slammed to the floor. Instantly, he leaped up again to stand with his legs widespread.

Godsamighty! When she had *gloop*ed the "Lazy" bubble out of him on her last visit to this Academy, he'd seemed way less fierce. Of course, back then he'd been quietly napping on a bench in an olive grove off the MOA courtyard. Now, however, he loomed before her, nearly seven feet tall. His arms were muscled, his hands fisted, and his intense blue eyes were blazing at her. Talk about intimidating!

Being the center of attention—especially of the powerful Zeus's *unhappy* attention—was not on her wish list. Not at all! If only she hadn't sent him that note!

"Who. Are. You?" he demanded, pointing a long finger at her.

"Me?" squeaked Elpis, bobbing farther away from him. "Uh . . . one of the bubbles you created during the Titan War?" she replied in a small voice. "Remember? You wanted trouble bubbles to cause those Titans to lose their focus in battle. So that you could capture them more easily. Great plan, by the way. Now you and the other Olympians have taken your rightful places as rulers of Mount Olympus."

"What?" yelled Zeus, slapping a hand to his forehead. "You're a *trouble bubble*? Not again!" He sighed heavily. "Too late, I realized that once troubles are created they can never be *un*created. They'll always exist. But I thought Pandora trapped all ten of you troublemakers safely back in your box. How did you get out?"

"No! I'm *not* a trouble bubble! I'm Elpis, the helpful 'Hope' bubble who *gloop*ed the 'Lazy' out of you, remember? You called me here today?" she reminded him.

At this news, Zeus calmed down. He cocked his head to one side, and then tapped his chin with a fingertip. "Ah! Elpis. Right! Just so you know, neither trouble bubbles nor 'Hope' bubbles can affect MOA students, teachers, or *me* ever again. After last time, I used my powers to make sure of that."

Elpis's eyebrows rose. Keeping *troubles* away made sense. But why keep *hope* away? Well, she supposed immortals and others here at MOA could magic up any sort of hope that was needed without her help.

"Anyway, glad you're here," Zeus said gruffly. "Because I've got something to say to you."

"You do?" Just then she noticed the thunderbolt on his belt buckle. *Hmph!* Well, she had something to say to him, too!

Before she could lose her courage, she blurted, "You threw a thunderbolt at a mortal family's house earlier today. Now they have nowhere to live. They'll have to rebuild. So, um, why did you do that?"

Zeus leaned forward, bracing both hands on his desk, his bright blue eyes angry again. "You dare question *my* actions? Me, the King of the Gods and Ruler of the Heavens!"

"No! I mean, sorry," said Elpis, backing away. "I didn't . . . um . . ." Feeling nervous, she began bobbing around the room.

"Not that I need to explain myself, but there's a reason I threw that bolt," he went on as his grouchy gaze followed her movements.

"O-okay," she replied. *Bob . . . bob . . . bob.*

"Stop all that bouncing around! You're making me dizzy," Zeus commanded. Staring hard at her, he moved out from behind his desk. After taking a seat on a front corner of it, he crossed his arms again.

"Ye gods! You have more muscles in your arms

than most immortals and mortals have in their whole bodies! *Oops*, did I just say that out loud?" she asked him.

He let out a rumbling laugh, and then nodded. Seeming to relax a bit further, he uncrossed his arms. His eyes moved up and down as he tried to focus on her while she attempted to slow her nervous bobbing. "Sorry, but I can't keep talking to a bobbing bubble," he said after a moment.

"W-what are you going to do?" she stuttered. *Bob . . . bob . . . bob.* Was he going to smite her with a thunderbolt? Or reach out and pop her? Or . . . yikes! Was he going to lock her back in that box? She glanced around the room but didn't see it anywhere. Still . . .

"Don't worry. I'm just going to change you into a different form for the time being," he told her.

"Different form? For the time being?" she echoed. What did he mean by that? Quickly, Elpis bobbed around to the far side of a file cabinet, *hoping* to hide. She couldn't help cringing at the sight of some big dents in it. Had Zeus punched it in anger at some point?

Unfortunately, her hidey-hopes didn't work. Feeling eyes upon her, she looked up. Zeus towered over the enormous cabinet now. He was so tall that he could see her just by leaning over it! He crooked one index finger, indicating she should rise so he could see her better.

"Ready for your new form?" he asked, once she'd reluctantly done so.

"Oh! Um, can we discuss that idea first? I mean, I'm used to being a bubble, so . . . ," she protested shakily.

It was as if Zeus didn't even hear her. He straightened, balling all ten of his big fingers into two large fists. Then he flicked his fingers toward her, throwing invisible magic in her direction. *Brrring!*

Instantly, Elpis felt herself changing. Growing bigger. And bigger. *Oh no! Would Zeus's magic cause her to get so big that she'd pop?*

But it wasn't long before she ceased growing. Catching sight of herself in a tall mirror hanging on Zeus's far wall, she gasped at her reflection. Because she wasn't a small, round, sparkly golden bubble anymore. Instead she'd become a sparkly golden *girl!* One about the same size as the goddessgirls she'd seen earlier in the hallway. The flowy chiton and sandals she wore and her long, wavy hair were all sparkly golden too. As she watched, tiny twinkly bubbles formed on her gown here and there before floating off to quietly pop.

Elpis's eyes (*real girl eyes!*) widened. "Wow! You turned me into a bubble-girl!" She lifted one sandaled foot and then the other, wobbling as she tried to walk. When she almost tipped over, she caught herself, grabbing on to the back of a nearby chair just in time.

"This is so weird," she said. "I'm afraid I'll fall and accidentally pop myself."

"No worries. I think of everything." Zeus tapped his forehead with the knuckles of one fist, as if to indicate there were extra-large brains inside it. Then he said, "I figured you don't want to give up your bubble form entirely, so I've gifted you the ability to shapeshift between girl form and bubble form whenever you like. While in girl form, you can't be popped. It's a safety feature."

"That sounds wise," she said, nodding in relief.

Zeus smiled at her comment, his chest puffing out. "Yeah, that's me—*wise*." As if in celebration of his wisdom, or possibly because he needed to work off some energy, he did an impromptu folk dance, whirling in a circle while rhythmically kicking out his feet and alternately thrusting his fists in the air.

All at once, he stopped, facing a window. "Uh-oh," he said as he peered out through the glass. "Hera's coming!" His eyes swept over his untidy office. Panic filled his face. "My darling wife is putting up signs in the halls and sports fields, requesting decoration ideas for the Winter Ball. Once she's finished, she'll come here."

Elpis nodded (for the first time ever!). "Okay. And . . . ?" she said, not understanding his concern.

His worried eyes flicked around the room again. "Hera organized my office a while back, but somehow it has gotten a little, er, messy," he explained. "She can't see it like this. Quick! Help me neaten it up while I give you the instructions you'll need for your time here."

"My time here?" Elpis repeated slowly. Apparently Zeus intended her to stay a while. Why, she hadn't a clue. But she found herself liking the idea. "Okay, sure," she told him.

They began working together in a rush. Pieces of an Olympusopoly board game went into a box that got shoved onto a shelf. Empty bottles of Zeus Juice went into the recycle bin. Half-dead plants perched atop file cabinets and shelves went into a compost bin. In her hurry to help, Elpis dropped things once in a while. She was not used to having actual hands!

"Now, where was I?" Zeus asked as they scrambled to bring order to his office.

"Um . . . the thunderbolt? The villagers?" Elpis asked, wanting to get some answers about the disaster she'd witnessed before he got distracted again. She crossed her arms. *Arms?* She had *two* of them. Again, *so strange*. So *awesome*!

Zeus's bushy red eyebrows smashed together as he frowned at her. "Ah yes, your message about my bolt. I received it on my way back to MOA."

Whoops, she thought. *Maybe I shouldn't have brought up the whole thunderbolt thing again.*

Zeus went on. "Trust me, I had very good reasons

for what I did." He tossed a small broken statue over one shoulder, landing it in a trash can without even looking. *Smash!*

Hearing voices in the office outside his door, he glanced toward it nervously. "*Shh!* No time to explain now. Keep working! That could be my dear wife, Hera, out there right now!" He tiptoed to the door, then cracked it open enough to peer out with one eyeball. Straightening, he elbowed the door shut again, appearing relieved. "Nope, just my administrative assistant, Ms. Hydra. She's out there arguing with herself."

The lady with nine heads, Elpis remembered. With that many heads, she probably had a lot of arguments!

Talking fast now as they continued to neaten things, Zeus eyed her sternly. "So I've decided what to do with you. You're officially on trial, with five days to prove yourself. It's Monday. So sometime on Friday, I will decide if you deserve to keep the title Spirit of Hope, remain in girl form, and continue sending out your hope bubbles as a permanent student here at MOA."

"What?" squeaked Elpis, bouncing on her toes (her *toes*!) in excitement. Was this why he'd summoned her? She could never have *hoped* for such an honor. "I didn't know you were considering doing that!"

"Only if you can prove to me, in a smart and thoughtful way, that you have the skills to bring hope to those around the world who deserve it," he informed her.

"I can. I will!" She wanted to do a goofy, happy

44

dance like the one he'd done earlier, but thought better of it. Her balance wasn't good enough for that yet!

Giving her a hard stare, Zeus nodded once. "We'll see."

Elpis scooped up a broken spear and tossed it into the trash. *Thunk!* She was mega-excited now, her mind boggling with all she'd just been told. Not only was Zeus *not* planning to jail-box her, but he was offering her a new job title!

If she could prove herself worthy of it. She had no idea what kind of proof would show him she was smart, thoughtful, and skilled, though. While mulling that over, she straightened some trophies bearing his name at the far end of his office. OLYMPIC CHAMPION RUNNER, read one. Another read OLYMPIC JAVELIN CHAMPION. And there were dozens more.

"Oh! Almost forgot. At times your job may require you to revert to bubble form. In order to transform yourself back and forth between your current girl form and a soap-air-water bubble, you'll need to choose a magic code word," Zeus announced.

"Huh?" said Elpis.

Zeus nodded. "Okay, 'huh' it is." He began flipping over the chair cushions so their badly scorched sides faced downward.

"What?" she said, feeling confused.

Zeus's bushy eyebrows rose. "You want to change your magic word from 'huh' to 'what'? Okay. Done."

"No! I mean, wait," she blurted.

"Make up your mind!" Zeus said, impatiently tapping the toe of one sandaled foot. "'Wait' is a fine magic word, but no more changes, please."

Understanding at last, Elpis mumbled sheepishly, "'Wait' is okay, I guess."

"Looks pretty good in here. Hera will be pleased," Zeus announced a few minutes later, gazing around his office in satisfaction. With a nod, he went over to his golden throne and sat. Now he turned his attention back to another subject: his two-foot-long sandwich. He lifted it from the plate on his desk and took a huge bite that decimated about four inches of it. *Chomp!* Bits of lettuce and bread crumbs bounced off the edge of his desk and fell to the floor. He was making a new mess already!

"So is that all? Should I . . . go somewhere?" Elpis glanced back at the office door. She still had no idea how she was supposed to prove herself worthy of being the Spirit of Hope by the end of the week.

After swallowing, Zeus muttered, "Go? No, not yet! There's another reason I brought you here. To learn . . . uh, what's that word? It rhymes with 'breath fix' or 'death tricks' or something."

"Um . . . ," she mumbled, having no clue.

Zeus's face lit up. "Ethics! That's it." He snapped the fingers of his free hand, causing tiny thunderbolts to shoot out in all directions. They smoked holes in one of the chair cushions he'd just flipped. "That's the other reason I brought you here," Zeus told her between chomps. "So you can gain an understanding of ethics."

"*Ethics?*" Elpis echoed. She tilted her head in confusion and promptly lost her balance. Quickly, she plopped down in the nearest chair before she could fall over. Moving around in her new girl form was definitely a challenge!

Zeus gobbled another bite of sandwich. *Chomp!* Then he explained: "Effix squeals with royal dimples. . . ."

"Um . . . what?" Elpis considered adding that he shouldn't talk with his mouth full, but then thought better of it.

He held up a finger, swallowed his food, and then spoke more clearly. "I said, 'Ethics deals with moral principles.' Principles that govern behavior. A moral code, values, right versus wrong, blah blah blah." He waved his free hand in the air as he spoke.

She nodded uncertainly. "Okay, I think I understand. . . ." Did he think she didn't know right from wrong? Of course she did!

"Here's an example," Zeus went on. "Suppose you wanted my delicious sandwich for yourself. If you were unethical, you might try to steal it." He frowned at her, tucking his sandwich close to his chest, as if he wasn't sure he could trust her now that he'd given her that idea.

He needn't have worried. As a bubble, Elpis had never eaten anything. On the other hand, now that she was a bubble-*girl*, she *was* enjoying the smell of his food, she realized. Still, she had more important things than food on her mind at the moment.

"I thought you wanted me to be in charge of *hope*," she said, spreading her hands in confusion. "Now you're saying I need to learn ethics. Why?"

Zeus leaned closer, looking her in the eye. "That's for *you* to discover. Remember, if all works out, I'll be bestowing an important job upon your shoulders!" After finishing his snack in two more big bites, he shoved his empty plate aside. "Don't forget, you only have five days to prove you're worthy of it. Now follow me." He stood, then led her out of his office and over to the nine-headed lady.

Elpis still didn't get the relationship between ethics and hope. And she wanted to know more about what he expected of her, but he wasn't giving her time to ask questions.

Once they reached Ms. Hydra's desk, Zeus pointed at Elpis and then said to his assistant, "I want you to enroll Elpis at MOA for one week, starting today. Send her to Ethics-ology, fifth period. Oh, and when my dear wife arrives, please send her into my office." Without another word, he zoomed off, slamming his office door behind him so hard that its lower hinge broke.

Well, that guy isn't weird or anything, Elpis thought with a roll of her eyes. As she watched the door swing crazily from one top hinge, she remembered something. Zeus never had explained why he'd thrown that thunderbolt. Finding out was the whole reason she'd wanted to come here! Hera hadn't arrived yet. There was still time to ask. But did she dare disturb him again?

Before she could decide, Ms. Hydra's heads each called her name. "Elpis! Elpis! Elpis! Elpis! Elpis! Elpis! Elpis! Elpis! Elpis!"

4

Ethics-ology

WHOA! WITH THE NINE HEADS ON HER NINE
long, serpentine necks all talking at once, Ms. Hydra
was loud! Elpis stared at her, unsure which head to
focus on.

Her gray head tsked, gazing at Zeus's broken
door. "Zeus doesn't know his own strength. I'll call
the janitor to fix it. Again."

At the same time, Ms. Hydra's sunny yellow head

smiled at Elpis, saying, "Congratulations! It's an honor to study here, even for one week. I suppose you'll take five classes each day, same as all MOA students?"

"Um . . . ," said Elpis. She shrugged the way she'd seen mortals do to indicate uncertainty. "I guess?"

But inside, she was panicking. *Five* classes? Zeus hadn't mentioned she'd have a full class load. How was she supposed to attend five classes, do her usual job of spreading hope bubbles, *plus* prove herself worthy of the official Spirit of Hope title?

"As you heard, Zeus wants you to take Ethics-ology," the gray head added, breaking into her thoughts.

"He has invited a special guest—Mr. Socrates—to teach that class here for this week only," the pink head gushed, seeming eager to share this news.

"This is MOA's Teacher Vacay Week, which means many of our teachers are gone till next Monday. Substitutes have taken over their classes."

"Ethics-ology will be held in the Hero-ology classroom this week," said her blue head. "And there'll be no Hero-ology class."

"Hero-ology? I know where that is. I passed it on my way here," Elpis told her.

"Excellent!" said the gray head, nodding.

Ping! Ping! Ping! At the sound of a lyre, Ms. Hydra's frowning green head warned, "That's the herald sounding the first lyrebell. Ethics-ology begins in three minutes."

The purple head eyed Elpis. Sounding a bit impatient, it added, "There's not enough time for you to choose your other four classes."

"Then what should I do?" Elpis asked, beginning to panic.

"Don't worry," the blue head said sympathetically. "We'll choose them for you. Hurry off to Ethics-ology now. Have a good time and make some new friends!"

New friends? Excitement rose in Elpis as she turned to go. She wasn't sure how to make a friend, since she'd never really had any, but she could hardly wait to try.

"Hold up!" the green head called to her before she could leave. Glancing at the other heads, it crabbed, "You'll need a dorm assignment."

Elpis whirled to face the heads again. *Yikes!* she thought, clutching the edge of the administrative assistant's desk. "Note to self," she murmured, "spinning around too fast makes you dizzy."

With a loud snap, Ms. Hydra unfurled a super-long scroll on her desktop. Her eighteen eyes darted around the list of names written on it. *Must be names of all the students who go to MOA,* Elpis guessed.

The gray head pointed to a name. "Apate just lost her roommate. We'll assign you to her room. The four textscrolls you'll require tomorrow for your first- through fourth-period classes will be delivered to you there."

"Hmm. That's odd," grumbled Ms. Hydra's green head, studying the extra-long scroll. "Two other roommates have already moved out on Apate in the past two months."

Ms. Hydra's yellow head ignored that and shot Elpis a sunny smile. "How convenient! Looks like

Apate's in your Ethics-ology class. So when you meet her, you can tell her you'll be her new roommate!"

At this, Ms. Hydra let go of the scroll, which promptly rolled itself shut. *Whap!* Now she made shooing motions with her hands. "Better get moving!" chirped the pink head. "You don't want to be late to class on your first day!"

"I definitely don't!" Elpis agreed.

Keeping her balance while hurrying down the busy hall proved no easy task. Elpis stayed close to the wall, so she could lean on it if she stumbled. The HERO-OLOGY door she'd passed earlier was just up ahead. But when she reached it, she noticed there was now a new sign posted over it that read ETHICS-OLOGY.

"*Phew,*" she murmured. "*Made it!*" She took a wobbly step forward into the classroom. Fifteen or so students were already milling around inside. Many looked familiar, and she quickly realized why. They were some of the students she'd helped on her last visit to MOA! The ones who'd been bumped by the trouble bubbles, which she'd later *gloop*ed out of them.

Hope rose inside her. She wouldn't be meeting them as a bubble this time, but as a bubble-*girl*. Which meant she could start fresh. Be an actual *person*. A person who could become someone's friend. In that moment she realized this was something she'd wanted for a long time but hadn't dared hope for. Hey, maybe she wouldn't make just one friend, either. Maybe she'd make several!

Looking around, Elpis noted that the many student-size desks in the room had been pushed outward, lined up against the four walls. An enormously long, rectangular table covered with a tarp stood in the middle of the floor. But where was the teacher?

Turning to search for him, she accidentally bumped into a desk. *Ow!* It lurched a few inches across the floor. *Screech!* Startled, she lost her balance and almost fell over. *How long before I get the hang of being a walking, talking girl?* she wondered. Luckily, though the desk bump might have bruised her, it hadn't caused her to pop. So Zeus had been right about that. *Sweet!*

Straightening, Elpis noticed that some of the students were now staring curiously at her. One girl in particular was frowning big at her from across the room. She wore her hair in many long, multicolored braids.

All at once Elpis felt shy. This strange and uncomfortable feeling almost made her bolt from the room. Being the center of attention wasn't something she was used to! After all, she'd been cooped up in a box for ages before going to live alone on a mountain peak, where she'd been invisible to everyone.

She wasn't about to pass up her first chance to make friends, however. So, staying put, she ignored the frowny girl and smiled brightly around at the other students. Waving in greeting, she practically shouted, "Hi, everyone! I'm Elpis! I'm new. I'm so excited to meet you all!"

At Elpis's enthusiastic announcement, *everyone* in the classroom now looked her way. Many smiled back, while others looked surprised or a bit confused.

Probably wondering where she'd come from and what she was doing here.

Wasting no time, she began moving around the room, introducing herself. "Hi, I'm Elpis. I hope we'll be friends," she said to each person she met. All appeared pleased to meet her, so she guessed what she was doing didn't seem *too* weird. Mission Make Friends accomplished! Well, mission *begun*, anyway.

Elpis got extra excited when she came across Athena. "Hi! Your dad—Zeus, I mean—summoned me here this morning," she told her. "Until a few minutes ago, I was a bubble. But after I got here, he turned me into a bubble-*girl*!"

Before Athena could reply, another girl came over to them. It was Pandora, the curious mortal who'd accidently let those trouble bubbles loose last time Elpis was here at MOA!

Pandora's face was scrunched with worry. "*Oh no!* You're a trouble bubble?" she asked, having overheard what Elpis had told Athena. "How'd you escape again?"

"I'm no troublemaker," she reassured Pandora. "I'm the 'Hope' bubble, the one who helped you *gloop* the trouble bubbles back into that box you opened."

Athena laughed. "Well, thank you for that. Being a ditz was *not* my style!"

"So true," said another girl who'd come over. Elpis recognized her at once as Aphrodite, the pretty, golden-haired goddess of love and beauty.

Aphrodite rolled her sparkling blue eyes,

saying, "And let's all try to forget my trouble-bubble-inspired armpit music, okay?"

Elpis smiled at her, liking all these girls immediately. When the trouble bubbles had escaped, she remembered Aphrodite had gotten bumped by the "Rude" bubble. At one point, it had caused her to tuck her right hand in her left armpit, bend her left arm, and flap it to play armpit tunes! *Frrrp!* So *not* her!

Now a pale black-haired boy wearing a dark cape with a skeleton-head clasp came up to Elpis. "Hey, I'm Hades, godboy of the Underworld," he told her in a rumbly, mumbly voice. "Just wanted to add that we were *all* glad when you bumped that 'Angry' bubble out of Persephone."

At his words, she recalled that Hades ruled over the shades (spirits of the dead who resided in the deep, dark, spooky Underworld). She'd once over-heard some mortals on Mytikas say that Hades and Persephone were crushes.

"You're welcome," she replied, nodding to him.

Then, out of nowhere, Pandora asked, "So, Elpis, if you got poked, would you pop? I wouldn't poke you, of course, but I mean, what would happen? Just curious." Without giving Elpis a chance to answer, Pandora rushed on with more questions. "Are you going to be a permanent student at MOA? Or just visiting? Are you mortal or immortal?"

Just then, that frowny girl with multicolored braids pushed her way closer. Two other girls fol-lowed in her wake. Elpis had met them earlier, when she'd gone around the room greeting students a few minutes ago. Brown-haired Zelos had introduced herself as the Spirit of Rivalry and silver-haired Koalemos as the Spirit of Foolishness.

"So can we call you Bubbles?" the braids girl abruptly asked Elpis. She smirked, and her two friends cackled.

Elpis wasn't sure how to react. Were they being mean to her? Surely not. Why would they?

"Oh, c'mon, Apate, be nice," someone scolded the braids girl. It was Aphrodite.

Apate? Hmm. Where did she know that name from? Elpis wondered. She'd met so many students now, their names were running together in her head.

Before she could ask, a goddessgirl with short, spiky orange hair pushed her way into the group around Elpis. The girl held a quill pen in one hand and a blank sheet of papyrus in the other. Poised to write, she leaned toward Elpis, an interested gleam in her brown eyes. "I'm Pheme. Since our substitute teacher seems to be late arriving, could I get some newsy tidbits from you for the column I write in *Teen Scrollazine*?"

Between Pandora, Pheme, and Apate, questions were flying at her. Everyone must be curious about her, thought Elpis.

Without waiting for Elpis to agree to her request, Pheme continued. "Now, I'm guessing everyone will want to know why Zeus summoned you to MOA. And why he turned you into a bubble-girl."

When Pheme spoke, her words puffed from her orange-glossed lips to rise above her head in little cloud letters before slowly fading away. *Wow! Immortals' abilities are so interesting!* thought Elpis.

But would Zeus be okay with her telling everyone why she was here this week? Basically auditioning to become the Spirit of Hope? Well, he hadn't said to keep it a secret, right? And something about this girl automatically made her want to tell all.

"Zeus brought me here to try out for the official job of Spirit of Hope," she told the girl. "I'm sort of on trial right now. See, a while back I was trapped for what seemed like for*ever* inside a box with nine trouble bubbles, until Pandora opened it. I've had time to observe those bubbles' bad behavior and think about how trouble can destroy hope."

"So, you're pretty much an expert on matters of hope *and* hopelessness?" Pheme prodded.

Elpis nodded enthusiastically. "Bringing hope to the hopeless makes my day. I just need to prove myself worthy of the Spirit of Hope job. Zeus is giving me a great chance."

Upon hearing all this, the girl with braids perked up. Nudging Pheme aside with her elbow, she stepped closer to Elpis. "How fascinating! I'm Apate, by the way, in case you didn't know. Please excuse my earlier rudeness. It really is nice to meet you."

Surprised at the sudden change in the girl, Elpis wondered if her value as a friend had gone up in Apate's eyes now that others seemed interested in her. Then realization dawned. "Oh! Apate! You're the roommate Ms. Hydra assigned me to for this week!"

"Well, *this* should prove interesting," said Pheme, scribbling away. She turned toward Apate, tapping the feather end of her pen on her chin as she considered this information. "You've had several roommates in the past few months, Apate, isn't that right? Why so many?"

Frowning, Apate replied, "Um, that's personal. Not *my* fault. Don't print anything about that in your gossip column."

"'Gossip column'?" Elpis echoed.

"Pheme's the goddessgirl of gossip and rumor," Athena informed her matter-of-factly. "She started out with one column a week. But it became so popular that the *Scrollazine* now publishes her articles any day she has news to share."

That word-puffing talent has to be useful for someone like Pheme, thought Elpis. *It must allow her to circulate gossip more widely.*

"Let me see what you're writing," Apate demanded, glaring at Pheme.

"Nope," said Pheme, tucking the sheet of papyrus behind her back. "You'll have to wait till it comes out in print like everybody else."

"Hmph! Are you even *in* this class?" Apate demanded.

"Yes," Pheme replied. "And for your information, I can go wherever the news is. It's called freedom of the press!" Just then, an argument between two boys across the room caught her eye, and she dashed over to get the scoop on whatever they were fighting about. Apate followed, still insisting that Pheme not include her in any news stories. Zelos and Koalemos went along with Apate.

Elpis was relieved when everyone's attention turned from her at last and the students began to talk among themselves. It was then that she noticed there was one person in class she hadn't yet met—a boy sitting alone at a corner desk. Hunched over an open scroll, he was sketching something on it. She headed toward him. When she got closer, he glanced up. It was that boy with the green-and-black hair she'd seen on her way to Zeus's office earlier. The one who'd been so interested in the Winter Ball poster requesting art and design ideas! Up close she could see that his skin shimmered lightly like hers.

When Elpis tried to peek at his drawing, he immediately folded both arms over it. *Hmm.* Why wouldn't he let her see? Did he think she'd make fun of his drawing skills or something? No way would she do that—even if he were the worst artist ever!

She pressed on. "Hi, I'm Elpis," she told him, waving her hand rather wildly at him.

He stared at her hand, then her face, looking back and forth between them a few times. Then with a deep sigh, he gave her a half-hearted shrug. "Yeah, uh-huh, I heard. *Everybody* heard. You're kind of loud."

"Thank you! I do try to enunciate clearly," she said, beaming at him. When he didn't say anything more, she asked, "What's your name?"

"I'm busy," he said.

"Your name's Busy?" she joked, playing off her earlier confusion over the magic code word Zeus had asked her to pick.

"No. It's Moros, actually," he huffed.

He must not have gotten her joke, she thought. She tried again, leaning closer again to peek at his scroll. "So, whatcha working on there, Moros Actually?"

Quickly he let his scroll roll itself shut. *Whap!* "It's just Moros. Not Moros *Actually*," he told her.

"Yeah, I knew that. I was only teasing." She grinned at him. "Must be amazing to be able to draw. I've never tried drawing anything. Not sure if these things would be good at it." She wiggled her fingers at him and laughed.

Moros just gave her a blank look.

"I didn't have any fingers till Zeus gave these to me today," she explained. Then she wondered if she should have said that. Maybe it sounded kind of icky? Hurriedly, she switched gears. "So how do you do it? I mean, with so many possibilities, how do you decide what to draw? And paint or pens? Tough choice, right?"

Yet another sigh came from Moros, but he didn't

answer her questions. Instead he stood up, saying, "Are you always this . . . ?"

"Awesome?" she finished for him. She grinned bigger. This boy seemed even grumpier than Ms. Hydra's green head! Something about him made her long to cheer him up.

He shoved his hands in the pockets of his tunic and looked at her like she was a very strange being, which she supposed she kind of was. Newly created bubble-girls probably didn't come along every day.

"I was going to say 'always this *bubbly*,'" he said. And, to her astonishment, he *almost* cracked a smile. "Where did you—"

But before he could finish his question, they were startled by an unexpected burst of loud music. *Ta-ta-ta-TAAAH!*

5

Socrates and Plato

EVERYONE IN THE ROOM TURNED TO SEE A mortal man with wavy, pale pink hair standing just inside the classroom doorway. He was playing a long, thin trumpet called a salpinx. A fancy flag hung from its lengthy tube.

Elpis moved closer to see what was going on, and Moros did too. Having gotten the class's attention, the pink-haired man lowered the salpinx. Then he stepped aside, making way for another, taller mortal guy with white hair and a white beard.

The white-haired man wore a wreath of olive leaves atop his head, a tunic, a cape, and sandals. Also, socks with bells sewn onto them! He strutted past the musician to enter the classroom. *Cling-cling!* went the bells on his socks. Stopping at the far end of the long table in the center of the room, he then whirled to face the students, his cape swirling out around him.

Throwing his arms wide, he announced in a dramatic, somewhat snooty voice. "I. Am. Socrates!" He pronounced his name as *SOCK-ruh-teez*.

"Bet I know how he got that name," Moros muttered from beside Elpis, staring at the teacher's socks.

Elpis let out a giggle at the idea of the teacher

being nicknamed after his silly socks. When Moros's dark eyes darted to her, she made a goofy face at him. He blinked in surprise, his forehead wrinkling in confusion. Maybe because he saw her as an interesting puzzle he couldn't quite figure out? If so she thought he and his secret drawings were an interesting puzzle too!

"No applause, please," Mr. Socrates went on, although no one had clapped for him. The students were all just waiting to see what he would do next. "Really. If you praise every astounding word I speak, we'll never accomplish anything in class," he continued, even though no one had praised him, either.

"Now, at Zeus's special request, I will be teaching fifth-period Ethics-ology here at MOA all week," he went on to explain. "You're lucky to have me and will no doubt remember these five days with me for the rest of your lives."

"Excuse me while I faint from joy," whispered Moros.

Elpis pressed a hand over her mouth to stop herself from giggling again. This boy was funny! And his sarcasm was understandable, since their teacher *was* quite pompous. Catching her eye, Moros's eyes twinkled a little, as though he felt pleased she found him amusing. She wondered what he would look like if he ever truly smiled. Cute, she had a feeling. *Very* cute.

"My words are as good as gold," Socrates went on, drawing her attention. "I can't spare any of my precious time to write them down, however, so—"

"—so that's my job," interrupted the pink-haired trumpeter. Hurrying over, he bowed to the class. "I'm Plato, Socrates' devoted philosophy student. I'm here to record his words, so that they'll be available to future generations to enjoy forever."

"This is mega-amazing!" Elpis heard Athena whisper from nearby. "Socrates and Plato both here in this room . . . all week. My two favorite Greek philosophers!" The goddessgirl clasped her hands together in delight.

Meanwhile, Plato rushed to sit at a desk. There he whipped out a feather pen and a blank scroll, poised to take note of every word Socrates uttered.

"This week in Ethics-ology, we will be discussing ethical dilemmas," Socrates continued. He began to pace back and forth alongside the table at the room's center. *Cling-cling!* went his sock bells. "And we'll examine the ins and outs of moral behavior." Now he paused, and his eyes roved over the students. "There are eighteen of you in this class. Before I go on, please divide yourselves into six teams of three." With a quick glance out the window toward a sundial in the courtyard below, he added, "You have exactly five minutes to do so."

All the students scrambled to do as instructed. Apate's friends, Zelos and Koalemos, looked over at Apate expectantly. Elpis recognized the emotion in their eyes. It was hope. Both girls seemed certain Apate would choose them to be on her team.

But instead, Apate shocked Elpis by coming over and linking arms with her. "Since we're roomies, let's be teammates, too." Giving Elpis no chance to decide differently, Apate added, "We'll need one more team member." Her eyes flicked from one of her two friends to the other as if trying to choose between them. Both girls looked eager. Would whoever Apate didn't choose have hurt feelings? If Zelos and Koalemos stuck together, they could probably easily find a third team member, thought Elpis. So wouldn't it make sense for her and Apate to choose someone else?

Her gaze scanned the room and fell on Moros, who'd gone over to collect his drawing stuff. He looked a little bored, acting as if he expected to be the last one chosen for a team. Probably none of his main friends were in this class, Elpis guessed.

"Hey, Moros!" she called out to him. "Will you be on Apate's and my team? Please, please, *pleeease!*"

Moros looked over at her in surprise. His eyes moved back and forth between her and Apate.

Before he could answer, however, Apate hissed at her. "Stop! We don't want *him*! He's the Spirit of Doom and Gloom! No fun at all. I've never even seen him crack a smile."

What? thought Elpis. She found Moros intriguing, funny, and smart. Plus, the fact that he liked to draw could come in handy for their presentation.

Before she could say so, Moros came over to join them. If he'd overheard Apate's unkind outburst, he'd decided to ignore it. "Though joining your team will be a big disappointment to all the others who've asked me . . . sure, I'm in," he said with more than a hint of sarcasm.

Then, looking at Apate, he added, "And, for your

sake, I'll try to be at least as fun-*spirit*ed as my doom-and-gloom title suggests." So he *had* overheard her!

Stifling yet another giggle, Elpis clasped her hands together and sent him her brightest smile. "Makes sense. Yay! So you're on our team. I was *hoping* you'd say yes!"

"Yeah. Lucky us," Apate snapped, looking annoyed.

"Lucky is right. Our team'll be great," Elpis said to Apate, meaning it.

For some reason, being around Moros made her happy, even if he was gloomy. And she thought his slyly sarcastic sense of humor was hilarious. Did he use that humor as a shield to protect his feelings, though? She recalled the look on his face as he'd read that Winter Ball poster in the hall and how he'd shaken his head at the idea of entering the competition. Did he think he wasn't talented enough? He seemed to assume things would go wrong for him, before they could *actually* go wrong. Some of the hopeless mortals she'd helped in the past had been like that.

"Students! Please gather around the table," Mr. Socrates instructed once all the teams had been formed. As everyone did so, Elpis saw that Pheme had joined the Zelos-Koalemos team. As she'd suspected, those two girls had easily found a third group member.

Once all the students ringed the table, Mr. Socrates whipped off the tarp to uncover a huge three-dimensional map. Painted statues about three inches high dotted its surface.

"Wow!" Elpis couldn't help murmuring as the teacher began to speak again.

Hearing the scratchy sound of an inked quill pen, she looked over to see Plato still faithfully recording his idol's every word. And probably every action, too! Occasionally, whenever Mr. Socrates paused to take a breath, the pink-haired trumpeter-scribe and Pheme exchanged a few remarks, most likely about the joys of writing, Elpis figured.

Bending close to study the table, Elpis noted that the big map was very realistic. In addition to roads and villages, there were castles with moats. And geographical features, too—the tallest mountain stood nearly a foot high and there were lovely valleys. Strange, scaly beasts peeked from the seas and oceans.

"What is all this?" she wondered aloud.

"A game board," Moros informed her.

"Oh," Elpis said in disappointment. She didn't really like games. When she'd been trapped in the trouble box, the other bubbles had often made up games to play. Games whose purpose was to score the most points. They'd cheated all the time, though, so it hadn't been enjoyable, at least not for her. She'd never won a single game.

Athena, who was standing nearby, leaned her way. "We usually use this map for Hero-ology class. We move the statues around for some purpose—depends on the assignment," she explained in a soft voice. "It works sort of like a chess game, only there are real consequences to the moves you make. Usually there are only mortal heroes on the board, but today there's a mix of mortals, immortals, and spirits. Interesting."

"Exactly." Overhearing, Mr. Socrates nodded his approval at her description. Appearing starstruck, Athena clasped her hands to her chest. Speaking to the entire class again, the teacher said, "This week, each of your teams will examine a different ethical dilemma involving one or more of the statues on this game board."

A hand shot up in the group. Not surprisingly, it was the curious Pandora's. "What's an ethical dilemma?" she asked.

"It's a problematic situation with two possible solutions," Socrates informed her. "And both solutions present difficult moral choices." Speaking to the room at large now, he said, "You'll begin preparing your presentations tomorrow, Tuesday. Then two teams per day will present their ethical dilemmas and proposed solutions on Wednesday, Thursday, and Friday, allowing time for the class to consider and debate suggested outcomes."

"That's not fair!" Apate objected boldly. "The Friday teams will have more time to prepare than the Wednesday and Thursday teams."

To everyone's surprise, Socrates seemed pleased at her outburst. Smiling, he held up his pointer finger. "Aha! Your first lesson in ethics. Ethical issues involve questions of fairness as well as moral choices. Life is not always going to be fair." He placed his hands on his chest. "For example, *I* am brilliant. Many mortals aren't so lucky," he said matter-of-factly.

Without looking over, Elpis somehow sensed

that Moros was rolling his eyes at Socrates' boastful words. *Tee-hee!*

"So! Tomorrow, at the start of class, you'll receive your ethical-dilemma questions," Mr. Socrates went on. "But for today, let's discuss a sample moral dilemma to give you an idea of how this assignment will proceed."

He began to explain, pacing back and forth. *Cling-cling!* "Imagine that a school friend named Nikos didn't study for a test. He asks to copy your answers. How many of you would *not* let him copy?" asked Mr. Socrates. When most students raised their hands, he asked, "Why not?"

"Because it wouldn't be fair to those of us who *did* study," Athena called out.

"What if Nikos was going to fail the class if you didn't let him copy?" asked Mr. Socrates.

"It would be hard, but I'd still say no," said Athena. Most other students nodded, but not quite as many as before.

"What if the reason your friend Nikos hadn't studied for the test was that his dad was in a chariot accident the day before the test? And his family was at the hospital all night watching over him. Your friend has been crying and didn't get any sleep. Would that change your answer?"

Athena thought hard. "I don't know. Maybe Nikos should tell the teacher what happened and ask if he could take the test another day?"

"Maybe he should've studied earlier in the week, though?" suggested Pandora. Other students chimed in with their thoughts too.

"All good responses," said Mr. Socrates after a

while. "As you see, ethical questions often have no easy answer." Just then the lyrebell sounded the end of classes for the day. "Your goals this week will be to work effectively in a group, demonstrate critical thinking, and offer a solution that persuades the class to align with your ethical choice," he called out.

Once he and Mr. Plato departed the room, students also began to leave. Elpis bent to study the game board. She noticed that all the little statues on it—immortals, mortals, spirits, or whatever—had been helpfully labeled with their names. That was nice. "So you represent real people?" she whispered to one group of little statues. "And our assignment is to help you solve ethical questions?"

"That's right," a tiny voice whispered back. It was

Moros, though. Not a statue. He'd come to stand beside her.

"Ha!" Elpis straightened, a little embarrassed to be caught talking to the painted wooden figures.

"The whole world will be watching our every move. Not to mention Mr. Brilliant Britches, who'll be grading us. No pressure, right?" Moros went on, shaking his head.

Brilliant Britches? It took Elpis a minute to realize he was referring to Mr. Socrates. She grinned, but then gulped. "Graded? I've n-never been graded on anything." After a brief pause, she added, "But I'm sure it'll work out fine."

"With that upbeat philosophy, you must get disappointed a lot," said Moros, quirking an eyebrow at her.

"What?" She couldn't tell if he was serious or just cracking another of his wry jokes.

Moros shot a glance at Apate, who'd wandered away to speak to her two BFFs. Then he leaned toward Elpis. "Listen, you should be careful around Apate. She's the Spirit of Deceit and Trickery. That should tell you what you can expect from her. Not everybody is as nice as you might *hope*."

She stared at him in confusion. His words sounded like a warning. *Should I take his advice?* Elpis wondered momentarily. His personality leaned toward being negative, so for now she would disregard what he'd said. She preferred to look for the good in every person she met, including her roommate *and* this gloomy guy.

Just then, Poseidon and another godboy gestured

to Moros from out in the hall. "Hey, Doom and Gloom, it's game time. C'mon!" Poseidon called, waving him over. Moros gave the guys a head tip, swung his schoolbag over one shoulder, and, without a backward glance at Elpis, ambled off to join them.

Hmm. Doom and Gloom. Just then, Elpis had a brilliant idea. (Socrates wasn't the only one who could have them!) To prove herself worthy of becoming the Spirit of Hope, she would seek out the most morose, grumpy, *hopeless* crankypants she could find around here and give them hope. It seemed likely that person was Moros!

Of course, Zeus had fixed things so that trouble and hope bubbles could never again affect MOA students or teachers. Even better! If she managed to cheer up the grumpiest kid at this academy without using magic, it would be a true triumph. Zeus would see and understand what a difference she could make to others. Surely he'd deem her worthy of the Spirit of Hope job. She'd get to remain a girl. Plus, she'd be helping Moros. A win-win if she succeeded! Yes, she decided right then—that boy would be her secret project. *Project Make Moros Smile!*

Little did she know that *she* would soon become the "project" of someone else, though. Someone who did *not* have her best interests at heart.

While everyone else packed up to leave, Elpis thought about what to do next. Should she go somewhere quiet and send some hope bubbles out into the world? As she moved toward the door, Athena fell into step with Aphrodite and Pandora. Once they were out in the hall, Artemis and Persephone joined them. Elpis watched longingly as, laughing and talking, the five girls walked farther from her to go somewhere together.

But then Athena paused mid-step and cast a look back over her shoulder. "Hey, Elpis," she called. "We're heading to cheer practice in the gym. Where are you heading?"

"Oh. Um. Not sure." Elpis cocked her head. "What's cheer?"

Pandora's eyes rounded as she gaped at Elpis. "Honestly? You've never heard of *cheer*? The best sport ever?"

Athena's blue eyes sparkled. "Our cheer team roots for the MOA teams that play all kinds of other sports," she explained. "And we do jumps and stunts to entertain their audiences."

"Yeah, and sometimes we go to competitions with other cheer teams, doing stuff like flips and pyramids," said Aphrodite.

"It's fun. Good exercise, too," added Artemis.

"You should come with us to see what it's all about!" Persephone suggested to Elpis. "Our uniforms are in lockers over in the MOA gym. I have a spare one I can lend you. We look like we're about the same size."

"Oh. Okay. If I w-won't be in the way . . . ," Elpis stuttered. Though a bit unsure, she decided to follow them anyway.

Athena grinned, giving her a friendly shoulder bump as they walked. "Great! Who knows? Maybe showing my dad you have lots of school *spirit* will help you win that Spirit of Hope title!"

"Couldn't hurt," said Elpis, both pleased and surprised that these girls wanted her to hang out with them.

"Are athletics really a good choice for a bubble-girl, though?" a new voice muttered in a sly, discouraging way.

Elpis glanced back over her shoulder to see that Apate was apparently following them. She'd sneaked up so quietly, no one had seen her. "It's okay," she assured the girl. "Zeus said popping's only a danger when I'm in true bubble form. Nongirl form, I mean."

"Oh," said Apate. The sly look on her face turned to one of disappointment.

Weird! thought Elpis. Surely Apate didn't wish her ill!

Just then, they all passed a sign hanging at the entrance to the gym. It read:

The Players' Pledge

1. I will encourage good sportsmanship from others and practice good sportsmanship myself.

2. I will treat coaches, players, and fans with respect.

3. I will remember that sports are a chance to learn and have fun.

This pledge is an example of ethics in action! thought Elpis.

Once they entered the gym, Apate peeled off to join Koalemos sitting in the nearby bleacher seats. Meanwhile, Elpis and her new maybe friends, Athena, Aphrodite, Artemis, Persephone, and Pandora, headed for the girls' changing room. While giggling and chatting, they stashed stuff in lockers and traded their chitons for blue-and-gold cheer uniforms. Two matching pom-poms were thrust into Elpis's hands. And then, suddenly, they were all dashing out into the gym to take positions along the sidelines of a court, where a game called Beastie-ball was in progress.

The other girls guided Elpis through their routines, and to her surprise, she caught on quickly. As they performed mighty cheers, two teams of students zipped up, down, and all around a hexagonal court, trying to score goals. Among them were Moros, Poseidon, Apate's friend Zelos, and a turquoise-haired girl named Amphitrite who Elpis remembered from her arrival at MOA.

All the players wore winged sandals, which allowed them to make quick turns and starts and stops while dribbling a ball. The object seemed to be to dunk the ball in one of the six baskets, which were each shaped like a scary beast (that growled!). Points were awarded based on which hungry beast the ball was fed to. As the Spirit of Rivalry, Zelos's over-the-top determination to win sometimes resulted in loud arguments with opposing players. At one point, the coach made her sit out for a while. "Not fair!" she griped, but the game went more smoothly during her time-out, Elpis noticed.

Meanwhile, Elpis shook her pom-poms, delighting

in the soft rustling sound they made. Joining the five goddessgirls in their bouncy routine was way more fun than she had imagined it would be! Though still a little worried about getting popped, in spite of Zeus's promise, she copied her new friends' movements, calling out the words to each cheer:

When the ball's released.

We feed the beast!

Slam-dunk it in.

May the best team win!

Before long, she was cheering like a pro. Arms up in a high V, or down in a low upside-down V. Thigh stand. Cartwheels and handsprings.

"You're a natural," Persephone shouted to her after a while.

"Thanks! Maybe because I'm used to bouncing

around?" Elpis guessed breathlessly. Not only was she good at doing stunts, she soon realized; she was also able to magically cause the small twinkly bubbles that came and went on her chiton to arrange themselves into colorful temporary shapes on her cheer uniform.

She covered herself in the large shape of a daisy, for example, with many yellow bubbles clustered to form a center. And many more white bubbles to form eight large "petals" fanned out all around. After trying several other shapes, she formed the bubbles into a bouncy kitten covered with little gray bubble legs, a tail, and a cute pink bubble nose!

"Me-ow-wow, this is fun!" she exclaimed, making her new friends giggle.

"Everybody's loving your moves," Athena called,

nodding toward a nearby crowd that had gathered to watch.

Whoa! What? Elpis froze. She'd been so caught up in her bubble poses that she hadn't noticed how many students were watching her. Including Moros. (Out on the Beastie-ball court, however, he was only able to send glances her way while he was on the move.)

"Wait!" she whispered, instantly making the bubbles disappear. Though she'd been enjoying cheer, she had no desire to be a *star*! Being the focus of attention just wasn't in her comfort zone.

Quickly, she joined back in with the movements of the other girls, so she was no longer a solo act. And all too soon practice was over. Cheer was a good name for it, she decided, because participating had made her mega-happy!

6

Shopping

AFTER CHANGING BACK INTO THEIR CHITONS, all six girls—Athena, Aphrodite, Pandora, Artemis, Persephone, and Elpis—headed out of the gym. As they walked toward the Academy again, Apate caught up to Elpis. Her friends Zelos and Koalemos were nowhere in sight. "Hey, instead of dinner in the cafeteria, I'm going to the Immortal Marketplace.

You'll have to wait around till I get back for me to let you in my dorm room, since we're stuck sharing this week."

"Oh." Elpis nodded, feeling a bit disappointed that Apate felt "stuck" with her. "Um, could I, um, go with you?" She wanted to have as many experiences and see as many sights as she could while in her current girl form. Just in case Zeus changed his mind and sent her back into that box at the end of the week. "I've never been shopping before," she added.

Aphrodite overheard, and stopped walking to look at her, her blue eyes rounding in shock. "Never. Been. *Shopping?* Then, yes, you *must* go! I need to buy some makeup at the IM—the Immortal Marketplace, that is—so I was going there anyway. I brought my swan cart with me," she added, patting the cute handbag that hung on her arm.

Now it was Elpis's eyes that rounded. Aphrodite had a cart in her handbag? And it could somehow take them to this marketplace? There were so many fascinating things to learn here at MOA!

"Ooh! Good. That'll save us some time!" Apate said, suddenly sounding more enthusiastic about Elpis going along.

None of the other girls wanted to go shopping just then, so Athena, Persephone, Artemis, and Pandora said "later" and continued on to the Academy.

After rummaging around in her handbag, Aphrodite pulled out a figurine of two snow-white swans that was small enough to fit in her hand. The swans sat side by side, hitched to a golden cart. With their orange-beaked faces turned toward each other and their necks gracefully curved, they formed the shape of a perfect heart between them.

Elpis eyed the figurine, wondering how it could possibly take them to the IM. *It must have some kind of magic*, she decided.

And it did. She watched as Aphrodite placed the cart on the ground and then stepped back, gesturing for Elpis and Apate to do the same. Afterward, she began chanting:

> *Feathered swans, wild at heart.*
>
> *Spread your wings to fly my cart!*

Instantly the two swans fluttered to life, shaking their heads as if waking from a deep sleep. Their wings unfurled, growing larger. In minutes the swans stood ten feet tall with wingspans of twenty feet! Aphrodite petted them, then waved Elpis and Apate to sit inside the cart, which now sparkled with splendid jewels.

Seconds later the swans glided smoothly away from the Academy, their long necks stretching ahead as they sailed the cart through the clouds. In no time, they were descending toward a huge crystal marketplace that sat halfway between Earth and Mount Olympus. *The IM!* Elpis thought excitedly.

After they landed, the three girls hopped from the cart. Then Aphrodite spoke another spell to shrink it, and she stowed it back in her handbag. They all headed for the IM's main doors.

Once inside the marketplace, Elpis stared up at the building's high-ceilinged crystal roof, awestruck.

Many, many tall Ionic columns separated seemingly endless rows of colorful shops.

"Wow, this place is enormous!" she exclaimed as the girls walked, turning her head this way and that to take in everything.

Apate smirked. "I guess it *would* be to you, after being stuck in a box for so long."

Aphrodite sent the girl a frown, but Apate didn't seem to notice. Elpis sighed. Her new roomie acted friendly one minute, but kind of mean the very next. It was weird.

She forgot all about Apate, though, when wave after wave of strong emotions abruptly began whooshing over her. A tangled mix of the invisible hopes and dreams of the shoppers and shopkeepers around them were coming at her from every direction!

Feeling dizzy, she rested a hand against the nearest tall column to keep her balance.

Aphrodite touched her shoulder. "Is something wrong?" she asked, sounding concerned.

"I—I can hear everyone's hopes. Dozens and dozens of them. Too many to help. It's kind of o-overwhelming." With her free hand, Elpis gestured at the bustling crowd. "I guess it's because I've never been around so many people all at once."

"Just ignore them," Apate advised, in a scoffing tone. "You're allowed time off the job, right? Besides, if you try to help *everyone*, you'll be here all year. Hey! Why not just send out a gazillion hope bubbles at once? I mean, couldn't you just sprinkle them around like snowflakes?"

Elpis shook her head slowly. "It doesn't work like that. First I have to consider whether a person's hope should be fulfilled. Otherwise, I could make their problems even worse."

Apate let out an annoyed huff. Seeming to give up on Elpis, she wandered over to gaze at some sandals for sale in a nearby shop window. Instantly, two clerks magically popped out through the window's glass and offered to answer any questions she might have about the sandals.

Meanwhile, Aphrodite stepped closer to Elpis, her sparkly blue eyes full of understanding and sympathy. "As the goddessgirl of love and beauty, I get stacks of letters from the lovelorn, and from those seeking fashion tips, too. Answering them requires careful thought. Just like your job."

"I imagine so!" said Elpis.

Aphrodite nodded. "I love answering those letters, but it's a lot of work on top of school, activities, and hanging out with friends. It took me a while to figure out how to take care of things and still have fun! And you'll figure it out too, in time. Caring for others is rewarding, but you also need to take care of yourself."

Elpis nodded. But deep down she worried that taking time for herself wouldn't help her reach her goal of becoming the Spirit of Hope. After all, she only had five days to prove herself worthy! And she certainly wasn't advancing Project Make Moros Smile by shopping.

Still, she was glad to receive advice and encouragement from someone who understood her situation.

She took several deep breaths, and after a few moments the needy voices quieted. They hadn't disappeared completely. But now she was largely able to tune them out, putting them into a sort of imaginary bubble in her head to be dealt with later. She pushed away from the column to stand straight again.

"Better?" Aphrodite asked her.

Elpis nodded again. "Yes, but for some reason, now my stomach's growling."

"I know a fix for that!" said Aphrodite. She called Apate over, and the next thing Elpis knew, the three of them were entering a store whose sign read ORACLE-O BAKERY AND SCROLLBOOKS.

All kinds of fancy desserts—cakes, cupcakes, cookies, pies, and other snacks—were on display in its bakery section. Elpis took a deep breath. "*Mmm!*

What yummy smells! And everything is decorated so cutely!"

An open archway connected the bakery to another part of the shop with numerous shelves of scrollbooks for sale. She wandered inside it as the other girls ordered snacks. Many of the scrollbooks had been autographed by famous Greek authors such as Homer, Plato, and Aristotle! (None had been penned by the super-famous Socrates, of course, since he wouldn't write his ideas down.)

"Want one?" Aphrodite asked, offering Elpis a chocolate cookie with sprinkles as they left the shop.

"Um, okay," Elpis replied. She sniffed the cookie as she took it. It smelled sooo good! She took a bite. "Ooh! It's delicious!" After quickly finishing that cookie, she took another.

"It will be invisible ink," a tiny voice whispered as she bit into the second one.

"Huh? Who said that?" she wondered, glancing around, as she munched down the rest of it.

"That one was an Opposite Oracle-O cookie," Apate informed her. "They tell a fortune when you take a bite, but it's always the *opposite* of something that'll actually happen."

"Weird, huh?" said Aphrodite. "Here, try some other ones." She handed over the bag of assorted cookies, and Elpis quickly gobbled another three. She'd been going to ask for more details about that weird ink fortune, but then she burped, surprising herself. When she looked up, the two girls were staring.

"*Oops!* Excuse me, please. It's just . . . I've never

eaten anything before." Hearing this, her companions goggled at her. She handed the snack bag back to Aphrodite. "Guess I'd better slow down," she said sheepishly.

Apate grinned. Punching a fist in the air, she declared, "Yay! More for Aphrodite and me!" Which made Aphrodite and Elpis giggle.

Moving on, the three girls continued exploring the marketplace. Elpis's head whipped back and forth as she gazed in wonder at the variety of shops, which sold everything from jewelry and flowers to tools, spears, and pet fish. She was starting to feel at ease in her girl form, she realized. And she was having a great time, too!

However, when they came upon Hera's Happy Endings—a shop filled with fancy wedding and party fashions—Elpis halted in sudden distress. Staring at the gowns in the shop window, she blurted, "*Oh no! I just thought of something. I don't have anything to wear besides this chiton I have on. I'll need more clothes for the rest of the week, won't I?"

Apate laughed. "Well, yeah. You can't wear the same thing every day."

"No worries. You can borrow from me," Aphrodite quickly assured Elpis. "I've got *two closets* full of clothes." She eyed Elpis up and down. "I have some things that would look fabulous on you."

"Wow, thanks!" Elpis said, surprised by her generosity.

Aphrodite lightly tapped a hand on Elpis's forearm and flashed her a bright smile. "Hey, what are friends for?"

Friends? Delighted that this nice goddessgirl considered her a friend, Elpis smiled back.

"C'mon," said Apate, urging them along. "There are more stores ahead."

Steps later, the trio stopped outside a shop with a sign that read CLEO'S COSMETICS. A sculpted bust of a beautiful goddess sat in the center of its large front window, surrounded by bottles and boxes of eye powders, liners, creams, and blushes.

"Oh!" Aphrodite clasped her hands together in delight. "They have a bunch of new eye shadows. I'll be here a while. How about if we all meet just inside the front doors of the IM in forty-five minutes?" She was obviously so excited at the thought of trying on all that makeup that she didn't even wait for a reply before she scooted inside the shop.

"Sounds good," Elpis called after her. Though she wasn't interested in makeup, she couldn't help grinning at Aphrodite's enthusiasm.

Until now, Apate had seemed content to wander through the IM. However, once Aphrodite left, the girl seemed bored. "Look around some more if you want to," she told Elpis, taking a seat on a nearby bench. "I'll sit here till Aphrodite's done shopping."

It kinda hurt that Apate didn't seem to want to hang out with her once the exciting and beautiful Aphrodite was gone. Elpis tried to tell herself it was okay. Those two had known each other a long time, after all, while Elpis had only truly met them today. And maybe Apate was just tired.

Before Elpis could decide where to go by herself,

however, Apate changed her mind. "New idea," she announced brightly, hopping up from the bench. "Let's go to my dad's shop!"

"Okay. Sure," Elpis said. Though puzzled by Apate's now-and-then friendliness, she followed the girl to a store called Be A Hero.

Once inside it, Apate pointed to a man wearing a yellow-and-black checkered suit with a name tag that read MR. DOLOS. "That's my dad," Apate informed her proudly. "He's busy, but I'll take you to meet him after those customers leave."

Nodding, Elpis's spirits rose. Apate's offer was a friendly one, so perhaps she *did* want to be friends, after all.

While the girls browsed through the shop, Elpis watched in fascination as Mr. Dolos used flattery and exaggeration to convince shoppers to purchase something more expensive than, or different from, what they'd originally planned to buy. He even sold a comb-and-brush set to a bald man! And a costly set of armor to a lady who'd come in to buy a simple hat. Talk about salesmanship!

Though his selling techniques seemed rather dishonest to her, shoppers appeared pleased with their purchases. In fact, there was a never-ending line of customers awaiting his advice and attention.

Elpis became so fascinated while watching him make sales that she jumped when Apate grabbed her hand. "Hey! My dad's free," she said, eagerly pulling her over to Mr. Dolos.

Why was this girl so insistent that she meet him? Elpis wondered.

"Apate!" Mr. Dolos gave her a quick, happy hug when the girls reached his side.

"Dad, this is Elpis, one of my many, *many* dear friends from the Academy," Apate said once her dad had released her. She linked arms with Elpis like they were BFFs, surprising Elpis yet again. Why was Apate so eager to convince her dad that the two of them were closer friends than they truly were? Was she trying to impress him? To make him think she was a popular student?

A big smile bloomed on Mr. Dolos's face as he turned toward Elpis. He rubbed his palms together eagerly. "Nice to meet a friend of Apate's! Now, what can I get for you, young lady? Plenty of items here to catch your fancy, I'm certain. We've got—"

Elpis interrupted him with a shake of her head.

"Sorry, but I really don't need anything except clothes. And I can see you don't sell those. Besides, I don't have any money."

Upon hearing this, Mr. Dolos's smile wilted and he seemed to lose interest in her. When another customer entered the store, he hurriedly told the girls to look around and enjoy themselves, and then he rushed off.

"But—" Apate called after him.

Too late. Her dad had already dashed over to greet the new customer. "Hello! Welcome to Be A Hero, sir. Can I interest you in a helmet? I have the one actually worn by Odysseus himself on his journey to the island of Ithaca after the Trojan War!"

"Really?" the man replied, his attention caught. "Well, I just came here to get a new spear, but sure,

I'd like to see that helmet." He allowed himself to be led over to a shelf lined with various fancy helmets. All were shiny and looked new.

Could the one Mr. Dolos plucked off the shelf to show that man really have gone through a war and come out without any dents or imperfections? Elpis doubted it. As she'd observed earlier, Mr. Dolos was more than willing to fudge the truth to sell merchandise.

She thought about what Mr. Socrates had said in Ethics-ology class. How ethics involved moral questions of fairness and right versus wrong. Was it *fair* of Apate's dad to coax people into spending more money than they could probably afford on things they didn't need? And on products that likely weren't what he claimed they were? Well, he

was a businessman. So his job *was* to earn money.
Still . . .

"Thanks a lot," Apate muttered from beside her.

Startled, Elpis looked at her in surprise. "Huh?
What did *I* do?"

Apate rolled her eyes. "Duh! Embarrassed me in
front of my dad, as if you didn't know."

Elpis blinked. Embarrassed her how? By saying
there was nothing here she needed to buy, and she
had no money? "Are you mad at me?" she asked
carefully. She really didn't know what she'd done
wrong. Were all friendships such hard work? Not to
mention confusing?

Apate's frown eased, and she let out a discouraged
breath. "No. Course not. Let's go find Aphrodite."

Still confused, Elpis followed Apate out of the

shop. Seconds later she saw a group of MOA boys going into a store called Game On! Spotting Moros among them, she waved. He waved back, but when he noticed Apate alongside her, he frowned before following his friends inside the store.

Apate nudged her. "Hey! I think Moros has a crush on you," she teased as they continued on to meet Aphrodite.

What? Elpis turned to look at her. "No he doesn't."

"Uh-*huh*. I saw you guys talking all flirty in Ethics-ology today," Apate went on.

"*Flirty?* No way!" Elpis protested. She wanted to explain that she and Moros had simply been discussing his design ability. But since he'd seemed determined to keep his drawing skills secret, she didn't. "I hardly even know Moros. And I've never crushed on anyone. I don't think I want to. I wouldn't know how."

Apate only shrugged, gazing at her with a sly expression. "Sure, whatever you say."

"Oh, look, there's Aphrodite," Elpis said, pointing up ahead. Aphrodite was just coming out of Cleo's Cosmetics carrying a pink shopping bag. Seeing the two girls, she waved and then gestured toward the exit. Relieved to abandon the crush talk, Elpis hurried to meet her there, with Apate close behind.

7

Crush!

"THAT WAS *SOOO* FUN. THANKS, YOU GUYS," Elpis told Aphrodite and Apate twenty minutes later as they all trudged up the marble staircase inside Mount Olympus Academy. And it had been, despite her uncomfortable experience at the Be A Hero shop.

Although they were only walking up to the girls' dorm hall on the fourth floor, it felt to Elpis like she was climbing a mountain. The sun had gone down, but it wasn't too late. Still, given all that had happened since this morning, it was little wonder she was exhausted.

First, while still a bubble, she'd helped a mortal family weather a thunderbolt disaster. Later, Zeus had turned her into a girl and sort of offered her the post of Spirit of Hope. She'd attended her first class at MOA, learned some Beastie-ball cheers, and flown in a magical swan cart to the Immortal Marketplace. Her exhaustion was worth it. Because she'd had fun and, best of all, made some friends!

However, what she had *not* done, she thought guiltily, was make great strides toward deserving that Spirit of Hope job! Tomorrow was Tuesday. She'd have to work harder on that over the next four days. Problem was, she wasn't sure how to prove she deserved the title. Since being released from the trouble box, she'd spent most of her time spreading hope. What more did Zeus want? If Project Make Moros Smile worked out, would that even be enough?

When the girls reached the fourth-floor landing, Aphrodite pushed through a door. Apate and Elpis followed her into a long hall. "Girls' rooms are here. Boys are up on the fifth floor," Aphrodite informed Elpis.

When they reached Aphrodite's room, the goddess-girl opened her door and invited Elpis and Apate inside. Elpis looked around the neat room with interest. Red and pink heart-shaped pillows lay on Aphrodite's two beds, and each bed was covered with a plush red velvet comforter stitched with a pattern of little white hearts. Bottles of nail polish, lipsticks in every color, and other cosmetics sat atop a silver tray on one of her two desks. Aphrodite set her pink shopping bag on top of her other desk alongside a stack of papyrus and a pink feather pen.

"What a cute room!" Apate said, sounding a bit jealous.

"Thanks," Aphrodite replied.

"It *is* cute," Elpis agreed. If Apate had never visited this room before, she and Aphrodite must not hang out together much, Elpis realized. So Aphrodite couldn't be one of the many *dear friends* Apate had mentioned to her dad. Fleetingly, she wondered if Apate *had* any friends. Besides Zelos and Koalemos, of course.

As Apate wandered around the room studying the decor, Aphrodite opened her two closets and began gathering the outfits Elpis would need for the rest of her week at MOA. Even though the girls were super weary, Aphrodite took this job seriously. "Gold and white look great on you," she remarked to Elpis as she held up chitons of various styles and colors against Elpis's sparkly golden skin and hair. Sometimes Aphrodite would shake her head and put a chiton away again. Other times she'd nod in approval and hang one over her bent forearm.

After making her final choices, Aphrodite handed Elpis a stack of chitons plus a nightie, and some underthings. "Here you go. Your new wardrobe for the week." Waving away Elpis's thank-yous as she

and Apate departed, Aphrodite merely grinned, saying, "Sure—happy to help a friend."

Elpis grinned over that comment as her new
roomie led her farther down the hall. Apate's room
was on the same side as Aphrodite's, seven doors on.
Once they went inside, Apate turned on a lamp.

Elpis glanced around. Although the layout of the
room was the same as Aphrodite's, with two beds,
two closets, and two desks, Apate's decorating was
quite different. She seemed to favor drab colors like
dull browns and grays. Definitely not as appealing
as the cheery colors in Aphrodite's room. And the
room was bare of decorations. No cute pillows or
feather pens.

Elpis jerked in surprise when Apate abruptly
grabbed the chitons out of her arms and quickly

hung them in her empty spare closet. Probably the closet where her last roommate had hung her clothes, Elpis figured. It occurred to her now to wonder why that roommate had left. Maybe she'd ask Apate later when she had more energy.

"I know my room's not as cute as Aphrodite's." Apate blurted out suddenly. "No one's is. She's fantastic with decor."

"Your room's nice too," Elpis said politely. "Thanks so much for letting me stay here."

"Hmph," Apate scoffed. She'd already started preparing for bed, shrugging off her chiton and changing into pj's. Feeling not quite welcome, Elpis went over and studied the shelf of scrollbooks above Apate's desk. She couldn't help noticing the many books about deceit and trickery, with titles like *How to Cheat on a Test and Get Away with It* and *Quick Tricks to Sell Anything to Anyone!*

Though Apate must have seen her staring at the books, she didn't remark on it. When Elpis turned back to her, Apate pointed toward the nearest bed. "I sleep here. You can take the other bed." So saying, she snapped off the lamp and flopped down to snuggle under her bedcovers for the night.

Elpis sighed. If only she could do the same. But she needed to make *some* progress toward her Spirit of Hope goal tonight. So she forced herself to stay awake. Luckily, there was enough moonlight filtering in through the window to see by. Quietly, she changed into her borrowed nightie, and then sat on a desk chair next to the open window at the far end of Apate's room. There she spent the next two hours considering and answering pleas from the hopeless and sending out hundreds of hope-filled bubbles to those whose requests she judged worthy of fulfillment.

"Hope," she'd whisper, gently puffing the word into one bubble after another before releasing them. As fast as she created them, the hope-filled bubbles drifted out into the starlit night.

When her head began bobbing forward drowsily, Elpis knew she'd grown too sleepy to do more. She was *sooo* tired. Maybe someday she'd be able to have a more balanced life like the one Aphrodite had suggested. A life filled with the joy of helping others, *plus* school, friends, and fun! She *hoped* so!

Just as she was heading to bed, two urgent calls for hope came to her. Both were from Greek heroes—Pericles of Athens and Lysander of Sparta.

She yawned. *Hmm.* Athens and Sparta. She recalled seeing those two locations on the game board in Ethics-ology class. They stood about 130 miles apart, near the Mediterranean and Adriatic Seas, and were the two most important city-states in Greece, both with many residents.

These two mortal heroes each sought to bring hope to their people. She blinked, trying to keep her eyes open long enough to examine their plans in detail the way she normally would. *Blink . . . blink . . . yawn.* Their goals seemed admirable. *Yawn. Blink.* Surely she could trust these important men to do good.

Yawning super big, Elpis distractedly sent each hero a hope-filled bubble. As the bubbles floated off into the night, she face-planted onto her mattress and fell into a deep sleep.

Little did she know that those two bubbles would not reach Athens and Sparta in the usual way. Instead they floated out of Apate's window, drifted downward, and then whisked inside the open window of the Ethics-ology classroom. There the bubbles gently bumped themselves against two statues on the game board. *Pop! Pop!* Instantly, the two real mortal heroes down on Earth who the statues represented were filled with hope for the success of their goals.

If Elpis had examined their goals more closely, she never would've sent those hope bubbles. Now it was too late.

Ping! When the school lyrebell sounded Tuesday morning, Elpis groaned. Rolling over in bed, she saw Apate standing by the door in her pj's.

"What time is it? Are we late?" asked Elpis, stretching her recently acquired arms high above her head. It was a delicious feeling to be able to do that!

"No, that was just the herald's wake-up lyrebell. Follow me. Showers and stuff are down the hall," Apate told her.

"Okay." Elpis leaped out of bed. When the two girls returned to Apate's room after showering, they found four textscrolls leaning up against the room door.

"These must be for you," Apate said, picking them up and handing them to Elpis. Inside, Elpis tossed the scrolls onto her bed. She didn't have time to look at them right now. They had to get dressed! Girls had so many chores, it seemed. Showering, dressing, brushing their teeth. Life as a bubble was easier (except for the risk of being popped). Still, she liked being a girl so far. Fingers crossed Zeus would let her stay in this form!

When they were ready to go, Apate held the door open while Elpis grabbed the three textscrolls she'd need for her morning classes—Crafts-ology, Spell-ology, and Science-ology. Then the two girls headed downstairs to the cafeteria.

Elpis followed Apate through the cafeteria line, eyeing the many orange-and-black clay bowls filled with various breakfast foods. They were being served to the line of students by an eight-armed, octopus-like lady.

"Ambrosia omelet? Some yummy yogurt? What can I get you?" the lady asked Elpis.

"Uh . . . um . . . ," Elpis mumbled back. She

didn't know what to choose, so she settled for copying what Apate got—the yogurt mixed with ambrosia, honey, nuts, grapes, and figs—and just hoped she'd like it.

Next, they carried their trays to a table in the main part of the cafeteria and sat across from Apate's buds, Zelos and Koalemos. The table where Artemis, Aphrodite, Athena, and Persephone sat together was only a few feet away. As she passed them, Elpis smiled and sent those four goddessgirls (and lots of other students) a wave. It pleased her when most everyone smiled and waved back. She really *was* getting the hang of this friend thing!

Koalemos shot her a look as she sat across from her. "You're popular all of a sudden."

"It's because of Pheme's article in *Teen Scrollazine*,"

Zelos informed the others. "It just came out today, so now everybody knows why Elpis is here."

"Yeah. They'll all be watching to see if you reach the goal Zeus set for you," added Apate.

Gulp! Nothing like peer pressure, thought Elpis, glancing around at all the interested faces peeking at her. Well, there was nothing she could do about their curiosity, so trying to ignore the looks she was getting, she began to eat. *Mmm.* Her yogurt was more than yummy—it was scrumptious!

While eating, she examined the three textscrolls she'd brought. Each was filled with a mix of rules, class descriptions, and information. When she unrolled the one for first-period Crafts-ology, an assignment magically appeared on it. She gasped in surprise. Hearing her, Athena looked over from her table and grinned, apparently guessing what had surprised her. Elpis grinned back. A nice shared friend moment, to be sure!

The entire week's Crafts-ology assignment was going to be to create various snowflakes out of papyrus. Students' resulting cutouts would decorate the hall all winter long. She'd never made anything, much less had it displayed. This would be awesome!

While skimming the next two scrolls, Elpis half listened to her three tablemates' chatter. Most of it was criticism of the others around them. They kept their voices low, though, so no one would hear the snarky things they were saying about them.

"That chiton Artemis has on is *so wrong* for her. It would look way better on me," muttered Zelos, eyeing that goddessgirl. "And . . . hello . . . wrinkles? I mean, has she ever heard of an iron?"

Elpis peeked over at Artemis. When she'd been bumped by a "Vanity" bubble during Elpis's previous visit to MOA, Artemis had behaved wholly unlike her usual self, concerned only with her appearance. Now she was the total opposite, back to normal. Though she looked cute, she hadn't gone overboard with makeup or worn a fancy chiton for class. Who cared if she didn't worry about making a fashion statement? Wasn't it more important that she be herself?

"I think Artemis looks great," Elpis murmured, which just made Zelos roll her eyes.

"Ooh! Is that a pimple on Aphrodite's nose?" Apate hissed in whisper-speak. She and her two friends craned their necks to stare at the beautiful goddessgirl.

Arriving at their table seemingly out of nowhere, Pheme overheard. She poked her head between Zelos's and Koalemos's and studied Aphrodite from a distance too. "Nope, not a pimple. Just a random pink sparkle that must've come from that chiton she's wearing," she informed them after a few seconds.

"Oh, too bad," Zelos said in disappointment. As Pheme flitted away, Elpis waved a hand overhead to dispel the words she'd puffed from her lips before anyone could read them.

"That would've been some good gossip, right?" whispered Apate. "If the goddessgirl of *beauty* had a *pimple*?" The three friends cackled.

Elpis frowned. *Really?* Laughing over others'

wrinkled chitons or possible pimples was their idea of fun? Again she peeked at the table where Athena, Aphrodite, Persephone, and Artemis sat. She wondered if criticizing others was what they did for fun too. Somehow she doubted it.

On the other hand, Apate *was* the Spirit of Deceit and Trickery. Plus Zelos was the Spirit of Rivalry, and Koalemos was the Spirit of Foolishness, so maybe they couldn't help how they were acting? Ignoring her tablemates, she lost herself in her textscrolls till breakfast was over. Then, as she rolled them up and rose from her table to leave, an unwelcome elbow nudged her in the ribs. "Psst! There goes your crush," Apate informed her.

Huh? Following the direction of Apate's gaze, Elpis spotted Moros walking toward the cafeteria doors with Poseidon and his other friends. Her cheeks warmed. She hoped no one had overheard Apate. Luckily, Zelos and Koalemos were no longer at the table. They must've finished eating and headed off while she was reviewing her scrolls.

"Crushy-crushy," Apate sing-songed.

"Shh! Someone will hear you!" Elpis said in alarm. "We are *not* crushing. Like I told you before, we barely know each other. Plus our personalities are totally opposite."

"Hmm. *Opposites?* Let's consult the expert," Apate said gleefully. Before Elpis could grasp her intent and stop her, Apate rushed over to Aphrodite's table.

"Hey, Aphrodite, quick question," Apate said. "When it comes to crushes, do or do *not* opposites attract?"

Elpis wanted to sink into the floor. Was Apate *trying* to embarrass her?

Aphrodite cocked her head, her blue eyes lighting up with interest at her favorite topic—*love*. "A pair who are different in many ways certainly can still be attracted to each other. As crushes, or as good friends. Often it's because they admire qualities in each other." Her gaze slid over to Elpis, then back to Apate. "Are we talking about a particular pair?"

Elpis quickly shook her head. She held both hands up, palms facing Aphrodite. "Nope," she said firmly. "I don't know why she's asking."

"Yeah. It was just a question," Apate added with a smirk.

Aphrodite's blue eyes fixed speculatively on Elpis. But all she said was, "Okay. Well, if *either* of you has more questions on the subject, I'm your goddess-girl!" Picking up her breakfast tray, she rose to follow her friends, who'd already headed for the tray return.

Apate clasped her hands together gleefully. "See? I was right. And Moros is definitely your opposite! He's grumpy and negative while you're all cheery and hopeful."

Could she be right? Elpis wondered. Moros *was* kind of her opposite. He always expected the worst, while she expected the best. Did that difference intrigue her? And him? Aphrodite had said opposites who attracted each other didn't necessarily have to turn into lovey-dovey crushes. They could just become friends. She could always use more friends, right?

As she was thinking this, the lyrebell rang. Elpis

was so grateful to hear it and be done with this conversation that she felt like finding the school herald and hugging him! Instead she said a quick "bye" to Apate. After turning in her tray, she shifted the three scrolls she carried from one arm to the other and dashed off to her first class of the day.

The sparkly, artsy papyrus snowflakes Elpis designed in first-period Crafts-ology were star-shaped, each with six points. She added cute happy faces and took them with her when she headed to her second-period Spell-ology class. This week it was being taught by a sorceress named Circe who wore jangly bracelets and was visiting from a far-away island. Circe helped Elpis use magic to make her sparkly Crafts-ology snowflakes dance in the air!

In third-period Science-ology, a substitute named

Ms. Khione took the class outside to create droplets of water and dust. Then she taught them a magic spell to shoot those droplets high into the atmosphere, where they became *actual* snowflakes! Elpis learned that snowflakes form when extremely cold water droplets freeze onto pollen or dust particles, thereby creating ice crystals. Then, as the ice crystals grow heavy and fall, water vapor freezes onto them, building up even *more* crystals. Although Elpis only succeeded in making one real snowflake with six odd-looking, lopsided points, she had the rest of the week to try again for a perfect one.

When the lunch lyrebell rang, she stowed her scrolls in her (temporary) dorm room and grabbed her scroll for fourth period. Downstairs, she hurried through the cafeteria lunch line, then carried her tray toward Apate's table. Abruptly changing her mind about sitting there, she veered sharply away before Apate and her friends could spot her. She wasn't in the mood for their snide comments right now. Instead she went outside to sit on a bench in MOA's courtyard. As she took bites of the sandwich she'd chosen—hambrosia and cheese—she became so engrossed in the scroll for her next class that she startled when someone spoke to her.

"Hey, can I sit here?" She looked up to see the dark-eyed Moros standing before her. He held a half-eaten sandwich in one hand. In the bend of his opposite arm he held a fat scroll containing many sheets of papyrus rolled and tied together with a thick blue ribbon.

Elpis nodded, set her scroll aside, and scooted

over to make room in wordless invitation. Right away, Moros leaned his scroll against his end of the bench and then sat down next to her.

"Eating alone?" he asked, taking a bite of his sandwich.

"Yeah," she admitted with a small smile. When his eyebrows went up, she shrugged and took another bite of her own sandwich, feeling a little embarrassed. After a minute she added, "I don't mind. Thing is, I'm not sure I fit in with Apate and her friends."

Moros studied her for a few seconds as he chewed. Then he swallowed and sent her a *told you so* look.

"Yeah." She sighed. "You did warn me about her."

His eyes twinkled. But before he could reply, they were interrupted.

"Moros! You coming?" Poseidon called from across the courtyard. He was standing with about ten other boys.

Gulping down the last of his lunch, Moros jumped from the bench and waved to the godboy. "Yeah! Wait up!" Then he glanced down at Elpis, "I'm off to play Episkyros ball."

Elpis wasn't sure how that game was played, but he probably didn't have time to explain right now. So, having just taken another bite of sandwich, she only nodded at him.

"Okay, well, see ya," he told her, and then jogged off toward the sports fields.

She was glad Moros's gloominess hadn't stopped friends from hanging out with him. Poseidon and those other guys must realize what a cool guy he was despite his demeanor. She hoped she and Moros were becoming friends too. Because . . .well . . . maybe he *did* intrigue her.

Gulping the last of her lunch, Elpis reached for her textscroll, intending to study some more. *Oops!* It slipped from her fingers and rolled onto the ground. As she bent to retrieve it, she noticed Moros's thick scroll leaning up at his end of the bench. He'd accidentally left it behind!

She set her own scroll on the bench and then reached for his, intending to take it to him. It was heavier than she expected, though. So when she picked it up, she lost hold of it. *Bonk!* It fell to the ground and its ribbon tie came undone. Loose pages of papyrus spilled everywhere and scattered, revealing a series of drawings of magically beautiful winter scenes.

"Ye gods!" she said softly. Kneeling, she studied and admired each one as she gathered them up. The drawings were amazing! Her favorite was one of mischievous twirling snowflakes. Their strange faces were almost scary, yet funny at the same time. Some of his drawings had notes written on them— suggestions for scenery, set design, and even how to organize and build various sets and props. These were clearly ideas for the upcoming Winter Ball! Was Moros planning to enter his work in the competition after all? She definitely *hoped* he would.

Elpis was chuckling over a drawing of a silly dancing snowman when a shadow fell over her. She glanced up to see Hades staring at her. Guiltily, she tried to roll all of Moros's drawings back together into one scroll before Hades could view them. She couldn't help feeling kind of protective of Moros, knowing how much he disliked others seeing his work. In fact, she'd had no business sneaking a peek herself!

"Hey—Elpis, right?" Hades rumble-mumbled to her. When she nodded, he asked, "Have you seen Persephone? She's supposed to meet me here in the courtyard."

"Oh, nuh-uh, sorry," she replied. Distracted, she loosened her grip, causing Moros's haphazardly re-rolled papyrus sheets to spill out again. Hastily, she bent to gather them. Hades kneeled to help.

"Whoa! What are these? Did you draw them?" he asked, admiring each sketch as he assisted her. "They're fantastic."

She nodded. "Yeah, I agree. They're ideas for

the Winter Ball event, I think. But I didn't draw them. They were accidentally left here and spilled out when I picked them up." Then, before she could stop herself, she blurted, "Moros drew them."

Oh no! Instantly, she wished she could take back the admission. *Just great,* she thought. She'd not only spilled Moros's art, but she'd spilled the beans about him being an artist!

Hades let out a low appreciative whistle. "No way!" Then he turned thoughtful. "Hey, sometimes I have trouble finding ways to keep the shades in the Underworld occupied so they don't misbehave. I wonder if Moros might have any creative ideas to entertain them. Maybe—"

Suddenly, footsteps pounded across the court-yard, heading their way. The two of them broke off speaking and stood as Moros barreled toward them. Before either could say a word, he snatched his sketches from them, then bent to pick up those that still lay on the ground. As they watched him in silence, he worked with quick, furious motions, stacking his sketches neatly before rolling them all up together.

After knotting the blue ribbon tightly around them all, he stood. Glaring angrily at them both (though mostly at her), he told Elpis, "These are private, *nosy*! If I'd wanted you or Hades to see my work, I would have shown them to you myself."

Holding tight to his drawings, he stomped off in a temper. Openmouthed and dismayed, Elpis watched him leave.

"Whoa! I've never seen Moros so mad. He's usually

pretty chill," said Hades. "Want me to go after him and explain you didn't show them to me on purpose?"

Ping! Just then the lyrebell rang, signaling the end of lunch. Elpis shook her head. "No, don't say anything. When I see him in our Ethics-ology class, I'll explain we didn't mean to snoop."

She could only *hope* she could make things right!

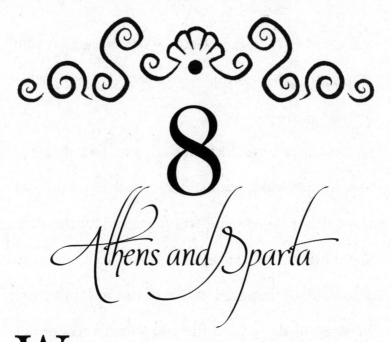

8

Athens and Sparta

WINTER-OLOGY–ELPIS'S FOURTH-PERIOD class—was taught by the goddess of winter, Ms. Kheimon-Horae. Today she led a class discussion of poetry written about ice, snow, and other wintery stuff. Elpis was so distracted by what had happened with Moros in the courtyard, however, that she had a hard time paying attention. She did manage to latch on to one interesting bit of information, though. She learned that an ancient Chinese scholar named Han Yin was the first person ever to note that snowflakes are always six-pointed!

On the way to fifth period, her feet dragged as she worried about how Moros would act toward her. Would he still be mad? By the time she entered their classroom, teams had begun to assemble. Seeing Hades, she waved to him before heading to the side of the game board where her team awaited her.

Elpis greeted Moros and Apate with a shaky smile. When neither smiled back, she glanced around at the other teams and then said cheerfully, "Oh! Our class has *six* teams—same as the number of points on a snowflake! Funny coincidence, huh? Or rather, *cold-y* coincidence?"

Apate huffed. "Yeah. *Hilarious.*"

Ouch, thought Elpis. It *had* been a pretty lame thing to say, though. She might not have said it if she hadn't been so eager to break the *ice.*

Moros just shrugged, his eyes avoiding Elpis's.

Hmm. Still mad, thought Elpis. She was trying to determine how to un-mad him when . . . *Cling-cling!* Mr. Socrates's noisy socks announced his arrival in the classroom. His buddy Plato followed him in, clutching a mysterious upside-down helmet in the crook of one arm.

They went to stand at either end of the game board. Then the teacher snapped his fingers. "Plato! Produce. The. Sock. Scrolls!" he commanded in a dramatic voice.

At this odd request, snickers rippled around

the room. These were quickly silenced when Plato whipped a large white sock out of the helmet and held it up for all to see. The sock bulged with something inside it.

As the class watched, he held the sock upside down so its opening hovered just above the upside-down helmet. He gave the sock a brisk shake.

Mr. Socrates gestured toward the six small ribbon-tied scrolls that fell into the helmet. "Each of these scrolls contains one ethical question and the names of the heroic figures—a mix of mortals, spirits, and immortals—that you'll manipulate in this assignment. Also the day and time of your presentation. Today your teams will begin preparing those presentations."

Good, thought Elpis. Once her team got their

scroll, they'd have to talk about it, and Moros wouldn't be able to keep ignoring her!

"Your team's first goal should be to decide on the most ethical answer to the problematic question posed to you." While slowly circling the room, the teacher gazed around at the students, his expression serious. "You'll guide your heroes' actions toward reaching a solution to that ethical problem. Though some may seem silly at first glance, these are *real* problems your heroes are experiencing in the world. All require swift, thoughtful solutions." Abruptly he stopped speaking and snapped his fingers again.

Plato, who'd dashed off to sit at a desk when Socrates had begun speaking to the class, now set aside the pen he'd been using to record his idol's words. He grabbed the helmet and carried it around the room, letting a member from each team pull out one scroll. "Also, if you need to visit your heroes on Earth for research at some point," Socrates called out to the room, "be sure to get a pass from the front office."

When Plato neared them, Apate pushed herself forward to pick a scroll for their team. Then she, Moros, and Elpis gathered around to read it.

"Our presentation isn't till Friday," Apate noted right away. She pumped a fist in the air. "*Yes!* More time to prepare! And here's our question:

> *What if two mighty Greek heroes from*
> *two neighboring city-states have opposing*
> *visions for how city-states should be run?*
> *Would it be ethical for them to encourage*
> *their people to wage war to make both city-*

states run the same way? Why or why not?

Please advise solutions for your heroes

where possible.

Moros noted the two names written on their scroll. "Looks like our heroes will be Pericles of Athens and Lysander of Sparta." He scanned the game board, then gestured toward two small heroes labeled with those names as other students got busy locating their heroes too.

Hmm. Where had she heard those two names before? Elpis wondered.

"Interesting," Apate added. "Athens and Sparta have been arguing about how city-states should be run for years, right? They keep trying to take each other's territory and boss each other around."

Elpis froze as she suddenly recognized the two names. She'd sent hope bubbles to Pericles and Lysander last night, encouraging them to shoot for their goals. *Uh-oh.* What if each hero's only real goal was to take over the other's city-state? By making war!

As Apate and Moros discussed their ethical question and how it might apply to Pericles and Lysander, Elpis worried about her hope bubble mess-up. Should she tell her teammates about it? Her eyes flicked to Moros. She doubted he was in a mood to advise her, not after what had happened in the courtyard. And she didn't quite trust Apate. Not yet, anyway.

So then, who else could she talk to for advice? Not Zeus. If he found out she'd sent hope bubbles to two troublemaking heroes, he'd *never* trust her to be the

Spirit of Hope. He might even stick her back in that awful box again. *Gulp!*

Maybe one of the four goddessgirls she'd hung out with after school yesterday could advise her? *Athena?* She *was* the goddessgirl of wisdom. Her wise words would likely be helpful. But she might feel obligated to get Zeus involved since he was her dad. Plus, Athens was named after her, so would she automatically side with Pericles?

Asking Aphrodite to help stop a war might pit her against her crush, Ares, who was the godboy of war. And Elpis didn't really know anyone else well enough to confide in them. So it seemed she'd have to figure out a fix herself. Without meaning to, she let out a big sigh.

Her two teammates turned to look at her, both frowning. "Oh! Sorry—I—" Elpis stammered.

"Stop daydreaming. We need a plan," Apate scolded. "Let's not waste time getting passes and visiting Earth. Instead I suggest we send a magic wind to each of our two heroes demanding that they send us written explanations of how their city-state's rules are superior to the other's rules. Then we can decide which side to encourage in their war."

"What? No!" Elpis gestured toward their two heroes on the game board. "Let's encourage Pericles and Lysander to work out their differences. Aim for a compromise in how city-states are run that benefits both Athens and Sparta instead. Peace is the ethical choice here, not war."

"Compromise?" scoffed Apate. "Yeah, like that's going to happen."

"Athenians and Spartans *do* like to argue," Moros

agreed. "If it's not about land, it's about which gods to worship or who's trash-talking who. It will always be something. They'll never get along."

"So we just give up and let them fight?" asked Elpis. "Surely that will do more harm than good."

"I didn't say that." Moros shrugged.

Apate rolled her eyes. "I don't care if it's harmful to fight a war or not. I just want a good grade to make my dad happy."

Poor Apate, always trying to get her dad's attention and convince him she was popular and worthy. Elpis kind of felt sorry for her.

They turned to listen as Mr. Socrates spoke again, clapping his palms together excitedly. "I see you've all located your hero statues. Excellent! Now, on your assigned date, your team's presentation should be strong enough to convince as many of your class-mates as possible to agree with your ethical choice. Because, after the presentation, they'll cast votes for or against the team's choice."

Apate leaned over to whisper to Moros and Elpis. "In other words, our classmates' verdict will pretty much decide each team's grade."

"Oh, and one more thing," said the teacher. "I suggest including visuals. They'll help engage the class and make your presentations more convincing."

A bolt of fear shot through Elpis, and she looked at her teammates. "Er, does that mean we'll have to get up in front of the class and do a *speech*?" she asked in a strained voice.

"Yeah. Duh," replied Apate. "What did you think it meant to give a *presentation*?"

"I don't know . . . it's just . . . I guess I wasn't . . . I've never done any public speaking," Elpis admitted, flustered. "Introducing myself to everyone here yesterday wasn't easy, and doing all those cheers in the gym was also kind of outside my comfort zone. Truth is, I don't like a lot of attention focused on me. I'm not used to it." As a bubble, she was accustomed to being invisible!

Moros shoved his hands in the pockets of his tunic and shrugged. "Makes sense. Not your fault you were stuck in a box most of your life."

Elpis sent him a smile. Unsurprisingly, he didn't smile back. But then again, he never smiled, even when he *wasn't* mad at her!

"No problem. I love public speaking!" Apate jumped in eagerly. "If you guys write the speech, I'll do the talking."

"Deal! I can do an outline of what we decide to say," Elpis agreed just as eagerly. Then without thinking, she glanced at Moros, adding, "And you could do the visuals we need—signs or magical displays—couldn't you?"

Apate cocked her head at him. "What? You can draw?"

When Moros just glared at Elpis, she sent him a *Yikes! I'm sorry!* look.

But then Apate protested, "C'mon, Moros, if you're good at art, it'll help our presentation. And our grade."

"Okay, but don't expect *real* art, alright?" he mumbled, caught. He sounded worried. Nervous, too.

What is it about him keeping his art a secret?

wondered Elpis. It really did seem like he had no idea how good an artist he was!

"Fine," said Apate, seemingly unaware anything was amiss.

"Yeah, that's really nice of you," Elpis said quickly.

Moros just grunted in reply. The rest of class went by fast, but the minute it was over, he stalked for the door. Elpis hurried after him. She had to apologize and explain about what had happened earlier with Hades! Moros needed to know that they hadn't planned to go through his drawings. It had been an accident. And anyway, they'd both thought his drawings were amazing!

"Moros!" she called out, stopping him in his tracks out in the hall. Heaving a big sigh, he turned to look at her as she caught up to him.

Spreading her hands, she looked up at him beseechingly. "I'm *so* sorry. I apologize for looking at your drawings without asking," she said, talking fast. "They're so good that I think I got mesmerized or something. I kept wanting to see more. But I didn't *show* them to Hades. He was just helping me pick them up after I accidentally dropped them. I think he got mesmerized by how good they were too."

Moros was quiet for a few long seconds. Then he raised an eyebrow at her, his eyes twinkling with humor at her word choice. "'Mesmerized'?"

Godsamighty! He honestly doesn't know how talented he is! thought Elpis. Well, at least he wasn't mad anymore. She wanted to do a little happy dance. Instead she just grinned and nodded, falling into step with him as they continued down the hall. When they stopped at his locker, she waited while he stowed his scrolls and schoolbag inside it.

"Where's your locker?" he asked her. When she explained that she might not be here that long, which was probably why she hadn't yet been assigned one, he looked unhappy. Because he'd miss her? Her heart skipped a beat. *Opposites attract,* she heard Apate and Aphrodite say inside her head. She pushed the thought away.

Getting him to do art for their Ethics-ology presentation had been unplanned, but it was a huge step toward ensuring that Project Make Moros Smile succeeded. Even if he wouldn't admit it or possibly didn't realize it yet, she could guess what would make him happy. Doing art and having it appreciated!

When Moros pushed some scrolls around inside his locker, two small sketches of what seemed to be sets for a theatrical play were briefly revealed, stuck to the inside of his locker. Casually, Elpis gestured toward the whimsical, amusing drawings. "How do you think up such fun ideas?" she asked. Although Moros only shrugged, she could tell he was pleased by her question.

"It's easy," he explained. He shut his locker and they continued down the hall together, heading for the stairs that would take them up to the dorms. "I just imagine things. Like *all* the time. Ideas just appear to me, so I draw them. It's like I'm watching a party or some event unfold in my head, with all kinds of wild and weird things that relate to a central theme."

"Those drawings I saw were ideas for the Winter Ball, right? So you're interested in designing *parties* in particular?" she asked, more than a little surprised.

"What? I don't seem like a party animal to you?" His eyes were twinkling again. But would this guy ever smile? He'd almost cracked one yesterday when he'd called her *bubbly*, but since then . . . *nothing*. It was becoming one of her top goals to make that smile happen.

"Well . . . ," she said, grinning. (Maybe if she smiled at him a lot, he'd start to mirror her expression.) "Maybe not."

"Fair enough," Moros said, seemingly unoffended. "But, see, a while back, Aphrodite gave a birthday party for Ares. I sneaked over and watched the whole thing from a distance. I've never had a party myself or been invited to one. There were lots of decorations, helmet-shaped balloons, and all kinds of stuff Ares would like. Anyway, from that moment on, I was fascinated with celebrations and entertainments of all kinds."

"Hmm. Since, like you said, you aren't a party animal, what do you think the appeal is for you?" Elpis asked as they reached the stairs and took them upward.

"The sets and decorations. Everyone's excitement when they first see them," Moros admitted. "In fact . . . ," he began eagerly. Then he stopped speaking and rubbed a hand over the back of his neck, looking away. "Never mind."

"No. What? C'mon, tell me," she pleaded.

His dark eyes studied her golden ones as they continued to climb the stairs. "If I do, you're sworn to secrecy," he said, his voice serious.

She nodded. "I promise not to say anything. Except maybe to Pheme."

His eyes rounded and he gasped. "What? Are you—"

"Kidding! I'm kidding," she said, gently bumping his shoulder with her fist. "I would never tell your secrets." Recalling that he'd thought she'd done just that when she'd looked at his drawings with Hades, she added, "Not on purpose, anyway. Honest."

They'd reached the landing in front of the girls' dorm. Instead of leaving her there to continue upward, Moros studied her face and then looked down at his sandaled feet. "Truth is, it's my dream to design events, parties, celebrations, and stuff like that," he told her. He waited. "Go ahead. Laugh."

"Design events? That's awesome!" Elpis practically shouted. "Why would I laugh?"

"Shhh! Someone'll hear." His eyes anxiously scanned the steps above and below them. But no one was nearby.

"Sorry," she said. Then she lowered her voice to ask, "So are you going to submit your ideas for the Winter Ball celebration? I think you should. They're amazingly unusual. And so *good*!"

"Thanks, but probably not," he said. "Parties are all happy and silly. I'm not, and my art reflects that. Others probably wouldn't see my quirky work as . . . well . . . appropriate for a celebration."

"Oh," Elpis said, hearing the disappointment in

her own voice. It saddened her that he might not try to make his dream a reality. And she didn't agree that others wouldn't like his artwork just the way it was. But before she could tell him that, voices came toward them from below.

Moros stepped back. "See ya," he told her with a quick wave. Then he took the stairs upward, two at a time, toward the boy's dorm on the fifth floor.

"Yeah, see ya," she called after him. Then she pushed through the door and into the girls' dorm hall, heading for the room she shared with Apate. There she spent the rest of the afternoon and evening doing her best to spread hope where it was needed, while her roommate and everyone else were probably off enjoying time with their friends.

That night Elpis slept badly, worrying about

last night's bubble boo-boo. How could she stop Pericles and Lysander from fighting? If it was war they sought, hadn't she already given each the *hope* that they might succeed at winning? She could move their figures farther apart on the game board to try to keep them from fighting. Or would putting them closer be better? Maybe then they'd talk things out? *Hmm.* Or maybe talk of war would just calm down on its own before her team presented on Friday! On this hopeful thought, she finally fell asleep.

Unfortunately, the next day was just as worrying as Tuesday had been. During lunch, the newest issue of the *Greekly Weekly* began circulating. As popular as *Teen Scrollazine*, but containing more serious news, the *GW* was regularly delivered to readers all over

Mount Olympus. And its news today was definitely serious. Fierce fighting had erupted between the two most powerful city-states in all of Greece—*gulp!*—Athens and Sparta. Everyone was talking about it as Elpis entered Ethics-ology class.

This is all my fault! she figured. A consequence of her sleepily sending hope bubbles to Pericles and Lysander Monday night. Those two heroes must've decided she *was* urging them to engage their city-states in a war! She didn't have time to dwell on a fix right now, though, because the first of today's two teams was about to begin its presentation.

The question Team One had drawn was this: *Is it ethical for an immortal to use magic powers in a contest against a mortal who lacks such powers?* Team One declared that immortals were superior to mortals and entitled to use their superior powers to defeat them. During their presentation, the team displayed convincing visuals as Mr. Socrates had suggested. They made their game-board figures—an immortal spirit girl named Proioxis and a mortal boy named Yantis—appear to come to life!

In a dramatic reenactment of an archery contest between the pair, arrows from both contestants' bows flew toward targets. *Whoosh! Whoosh!* Proioxis had magical powers, so, after ten rounds, she won the first contest easily.

However, in a second contest, which disallowed the use of magic, Yantis defeated her in seven of ten rounds. "Aha!" he called to Proioxis. "You only beat me in the first contest because your magic assisted you. But now I've beat you in a *fair* contest.

Therefore, I—a mortal—am the superior archer!" he claimed.

"Wrong!" called Proioxis. "In a fair contest, archers may use *all* their skills. Magic is a part of me—like my voice or my foot. It's an ability I was born with, given to me by the gods of Olympus. Therefore, I claim to be the superior archer based on our first contest!"

The team's reenactment of the incident had been an exciting visual. But at this point Hades—one of the team's presenters—quickly waved a hand over the pair on the game board, magically causing both archers to go still again. A lengthy debate among the students followed, as to whether immortals' use of magic in contests with mortals really was the most ethical choice, as Team One claimed. Then it was time for a verdict.

Out of the fifteen students not on Team One, twelve agreed with Team One's position that immortals should be allowed to use magic. The three who didn't agree (including Elpis) thought that magic *did* give immortals an unfair edge and was therefore unethical to use in the contest. Though her choice didn't win, it was a thrilling debate that got everyone thinking about fairness.

Team Two's question was this: *Is it ethical to encourage someone to pursue a goal that's likely unattainable?* This team, made up of Zelos, Koalemos, and Pheme, believed the answer was yes. Their two mortal figures—one man and one woman, named Theo and Daphne—had each decided to pursue the goal of becoming ruler of Rhodes, their city-state and an important trading port. The team displayed images of both mortals giving speeches atop a large wooden sailing ship.

Theo was physically strong and forceful, but not very intelligent. During his speech, he lifted weights and made up a slogan that said, "Don't WEIGHT! Vote for me!"

Daphne was smart and energetic, but not well-trained in governing. During her speech, the audience appeared to grow bored when she used difficult words that many didn't understand.

Both seemed likely to fail at getting elected, but Team Two concluded it was ethical to encourage them both, even though there were more qualified, likable candidates. Since the election on Earth would not take place until tomorrow, the class voted on the presentation without knowing which candidate would actually become ruler.

This time, the verdict was close. Eight votes in support of Team Two's choice, and seven against. The yes voters (including Elpis) believed most goals were attainable through enough hard work and determination. However the no voters thought that encouraging those who had little chance of success was unkind and a waste of time.

"The first two teams did great," Elpis remarked after class.

Moros nodded. "Fingers crossed we do as well."

"They weren't *that* great," Apate insisted.

Just then Mr. Socrates came over to their group. "As you've no doubt heard, the *Greekly Weekly* has trumpeted the news that trouble is brewing between

Athens and Sparta. This tense situation has stirred keen interest in those city-states, which means you'll be in a good position for an outstanding grade if you prepare a persuasive response to your ethical question. Let's just hope a real war doesn't break out!"

Elpis nodded nervously, while Apate smiled. Moros nodded too. (Solemnly, of course.)

As they filed into the hall after class, Elpis was worried. If Athens and Sparta's troubles worsened, she'd be forced to tell Zeus about her bubble boo-boo of two nights ago. And then there would be consequences. No Spirit of Hope title for her. Instead, possible *boxdom* forever! And those were just the consequences for *her*. She'd put many mortals in grave danger by unintentionally motivating Pericles and Lysander to wage war. In short, she'd created an *un*ethical situation!

Unsure what to do about it, she silently posed three ethical questions to herself: *Should I tell Zeus I made a mistake and ask him to help me fix it? Or should I let Pericles and Lysander duke it out and pretend I never encouraged them? Or should I try to fix my bubble mistake myself before Zeus finds out?*

None of these choices were appealing. With a shudder, she tried to imagine herself going into Zeus's office and saying, "Hey there, Zeus! Funny thing happened . . . I accidentally sent hope bubbles to two mortal heroes, causing each one to think he could win a war against the other."

Nuh-uh. No way would she dare. Maybe this whole problem would go away on its own, she told herself *hopefully*.

9

Moros Mopes, Elpis Hopes

. . . **NOPE! ON THURSDAY, NEWS CIRCULATED THAT** arguments between Athens and Sparta were becoming worse, causing trouble in the Mediterranean and Adriatic Seas. By third period, the fighting was being called the Peloponnesian War (after a peninsula in southern Greece). Though no one had been hurt yet, concern was growing.

Elpis had to take action, and fast, to stop the fighting.

That would lead to a happy outcome, as in no war! Plus it might prove to Zeus that the hope she brought others could get results.

Quickly, she came up with a plan. While everyone else was at lunch, she entered the Ethics-ology classroom. There she carefully moved her team's two small hero figures from their original places on the game board to a spot halfway between Athens and Sparta, setting them down face-to-face. She'd seen other teams do this, and hoped she was doing it right!

Since the little statues of Pericles and Lysander were only representations of the real heroes, she'd need to visit them in person to speak to them. Which would be easier now that she'd relocated them. Mr. Plato had said students could obtain passes to

Earth for research, so her next stop was the front office. There the very busy Ms. Hydra handed her a pass, no questions asked.

With the pass in her pocket, Elpis rushed down the hall and outside to the courtyard. As her feet flew over the marble tiles, she murmured the magic code word she'd (sort of) chosen for herself in Zeus's office: "Wait!"

Instantly, she shrank to become a small bubble. Since she'd been a girl for several days now, the switch felt weird. Yet in some ways she'd missed the simplicity of being a round, featureless creature. Because life as an actual girl was turning out to be much more complicated than she could've imagined!

She called up a magic wind, saying:

Magic breeze, come take me, please,

to meet Lysander and Pericles!

Whoosh! She was off, bobbing through fluffy clouds high above mountains, streams, and fields. Half an hour later, she was relieved to spy Pericles and Lysander below, standing precisely where she'd placed them.

"Thank you, I can manage from here," she told the wind. It whooshed off, and Elpis bobbled her way down toward the ground. *Uh-oh!* As she approached the two heroes, she noted the angry expressions on their faces. They were arguing.

"Shut up! I, Lysander of Sparta, declare that the City-States Theater Guild must put on a *tragic* play for the upcoming Greek Winter Festival," she heard that hero yell. "And actors from all city-states who take part in the guild's play must wear red costumes. It's the trusted color of Greek anemones and brave hearts!"

"*You* shut up!" Pericles fired back. "Comedies are way more popular. They'll attract more attendance. And everybody knows blue is superior to red. It's the color of Greek hyacinth flowers and of the sky, where Zeus flies on Pegasus. Therefore it's the color that must be worn in our theatrical *comedy*!

"No surprise you'd choose red. Because you're from Sparta. So not that *smarta*," Pericles added, laughing in a mean way.

Lysander clenched his fists, retorting, "Well, you're from Athens. Where dumb stuff happens."

"Talk about dumb. That doesn't even rhyme!" Pericles shot back.

199

"Well, 'smarta' isn't a word! So there!" shouted Lysander.

"Comedy!" said Pericles, snarling in Lysander's face.

"Tragedy!" Lysander argued.

Clang! Both heroes drew their swords, ready to battle.

Really? They were going to fight over a *play* their guild was putting on? How silly! "Hey! Stop!" Elpis called out to them, bobbing closer. They didn't notice her. *Oh!* That was because she was still a bouncy bubble neither could see or hear.

"Wait!" she called. Her magic code word instantly turned her from a bubble to a girl again. The two men clutched their swords and backed away from her, huddling together now and looking fearful.

"What is she?" Pericles whispered to Lysander.

"Not sure," Lysander replied. "Her skin doesn't sparkle quite as brightly as that of a goddess, but clearly she has magic."

"M-maybe she's an e-evil enchantress?" Pericles stuttered in alarm.

"No!" Elpis told them. "I'm the, uh, Spirit of Hope. At least I might be if Zeus decides . . . um, never mind," she blurted nervously. A lot was at stake here, but explaining everything to these two heroes would probably only confuse them. Actually, judging from the looks on their faces, they were *already* confused.

"I'm here because I made a big mistake," she admitted. "Last Monday night, you each made a hopeful wish, remember?"

Both heroes nodded, looking surprised that she knew about that.

"Because it was late and I was tired when your wishes came to me, I didn't review them carefully. I didn't understand that you were both planning for war." She paused and then sighed. "So I sent invisible bubbles of hope to you both." She looked from one to the other. "I magicked you here today to explain that it was wrong of me to encourage you. In fact, you should consider yourself winners if you *don't* fight. Instead, try to settle your differences peacefully. Okay?"

When the hero duo just crossed their arms and frowned at her, Elpis tried again. "So what's the big deal? Red? Blue? Who cares? Why not mix them together and make purple costumes? Tragedy?

Comedy? Maybe make your play a bit of both? Call it a Tramedy. Or a Tragee-com! Problem solved."

Both heroes gasped in shock. "Purple? Tramedy? *Tragee-com?*" they chorused. It was like she'd suggested they roll around in mud or something.

"No way! Red rules! As do tragedies," blasted Lysander.

"Blue is best! As are comedies," Pericles roared.

They faced off, appearing ready to fight again.

"Wait!" she shouted. Unfortunately that turned her back into a bubble! *Argh!* "Wait!" she yelled again. She returned to girl form. Her boo-boo had caused them to stop fighting. But now they were gaping at her.

Their argument was so silly that Elpis wanted to roll her eyes. Still, she could tell that these matters were important to them. Therefore she would pretend to take them seriously.

"I see your problem. But in war no one ever truly wins," she told them. "City-states are destroyed. Mortals get hurt. There are better ways—"

She was interrupted by a gentle flapping sound. "What's going on here!" demanded a familiar voice.

Elpis whipped around in time to see Moros, winged sandals flapping, land a few feet away. "Moros? You're here? How . . . ?"

"I saw you turn yourself into a bubble and blow away," he said, shrugging off his schoolbag and dropping it to the ground. "So I got an Earth pass and followed you. What are you doing here?"

Caught, Elpis admitted the truth. "I accidentally sent these guys hope bubbles, and now they're using them as an excuse to make war for their city-states," she said in a rush.

Moros's eyes went wide. Obviously he knew she could be in big trouble for this. "What can I do to help?" he asked her.

Before Elpis could reply, Pericles eyed Moros, demanding, "Who are you?"

In that moment Elpis got an idea. She *hoped* it was a good one. "Surely you've heard of Moros the Magnificent?" she said to the two heroes. "He's only the most celebrated artist and theater set designer *ever*!"

"Oh! Yes! I've heard of you," Pericles rushed to tell Moros, though Elpis was pretty certain that wasn't true. Especially since she'd made up Moros's new title on the spot!

Not to be outdone, Lysander exclaimed, "I've known of his work way longer than you have!"

"Hmm," said Elpis. "Tell you what. If you two agree to cooperate, I bet the magnificent Moros will consider whipping up some quick designs for costumes and a basic set for your theater guild's play." She glanced over at Moros and winked. "Right?"

Moros caught on fast. He nodded. "Deal?" he asked the two feuding heroes.

"Deal!" they chorused eagerly.

"All right, then," said Moros. After fishing a fresh papyrus scroll and some pens from his schoolbag, he went to sit on a nearby boulder. Pericles and Lysander followed him to explain what they needed.

Pleased that Moros seemed okay with her mentioning his art skills in order to calm these heroes, Elpis watched as he listened to them, nodding from time to time while sketching. The costumes he sketched out and colored turned out to be a clever blend of both blue and red. And the idea for a tragedy-comedy blend appeared to be growing on the heroes too, inspired by Moros's ideas. By the time he finished his drawings, Pericles and Lysander were all smiles.

"When we return to Mount Olympus Academy, we'll move you both back to your city-states on the game board," Elpis told the heroes. "And you will keep the peace. Agreed?"

"Academy? Game board?" the heroes echoed, sounding puzzled.

"*Oops!* Forget I mentioned that," Elpis said in a rush. "It's nothing you need to know about. So you'll remain peaceful?"

"I will if he will," Pericles said, looking at Lysander.

"I will if you will," Lysander blurted back.

"Let's see you shake hands on it," Elpis said quickly, before their agreement could turn into an argument. "Moros will draw a picture of your hand-shake. You can hang it in your theater as proof of your peaceful intent." Then, glancing at Moros uncertainly, she added, "Uh . . . right?"

To her delight, he nodded easily. The heroes smiled big at the idea of their likenesses being captured by a famous artist. "Awesome!" they both shouted.

When Moros handed over their finished hand-shake portrait, they approved it wholeheartedly. While they continued admiring his theatrical designs, Moros nudged Elpis with his elbow. "I think we're done here. Let's go."

"Okay," she agreed. "You go on ahead. I'll need to change myself into a bubble and summon a magic wind."

"No you won't," he said as he reached into his schoolbag. To her surprise, he pulled an extra pair of winged sandals from the bag. "You'll get back faster with these."

"You brought those for me?" she asked, taking them. "Thanks, that was really nice."

"Uh-huh. That's me—*nice*," he said, raising an eyebrow at her. "You left the Academy as a bubble, so I knew you didn't have any with you."

"I've never used them. How do they work?" she wondered in excitement.

"Only one way to find out," he told her.

Elpis darted over to sit on the boulder he'd vacated

and quickly slipped the sandals on. Instantly, their straps twined around her ankles.

Startled, she tried to stand and nearly fell over when the silver wings at her heels began to flap. "Whoa!" she yelped as they lifted her six inches off the ground. Her arms whirled in circles as she tried to find her balance.

Then Moros reached out to her and linked his fingers with hers. "Better hang on to me till you get used to flying," he advised. Nodding, Elpis felt her cheeks redden as they immediately soared upward. She couldn't help it. Because this cute boy she sort of maybe liked was *holding her hand*!

As they flew toward the Academy, her long golden hair fluttered behind her in the breeze. Her wobbles eventually lessened, and she grinned over at him. "I think I'm getting the hang of this!"

"You're doing great," he said, studying her balance. "But keep hold of my hand anyway, just in case."

She smiled big at him, nodding. Feeling good about having solved the Pericles-Lysander problem, Elpis was emboldened to move Project Make Moros Smile forward as well. It seemed a good time while they were alone. Before she could think how to further her project, though, Moros spoke up, "Why are you always so happy?"

Elpis smiled even bigger at him. "Why are you always so mopey?"

"Asked you first," he shot back.

"Asked you second," she teased.

Moros let out the biggest sigh in the history of sighs. "Fine. Honestly?" he answered. "It's sometimes because I start thinking about past mistakes. Things I did or said that I wish I hadn't. Or things I didn't do or say that I wish I had. My various mess-ups."

"Ah!" she said, nodding wisely at him. "Sounds like a case of *coulda, woulda, shoulda*."

"Huh?" He wrinkled his nose, cocking his head to one side. Which was super cute!

"You're so busy dwelling on things you think you could have, would have, or should have done differently that you make yourself unhappy," she explained.

Moros flung his free arm outward. "Exactly!"

"But what about all the great things you *have* done?" she asked. "Give yourself some credit. Today you helped me prevent a war. That's huge!"

Moros shrugged, still unconvinced. But she could tell he was listening.

"Nobody's perfect, right?" she went on. "Maybe the expectations you've set for yourself are too high. Beating yourself up when you fail to meet them probably isn't helpful." Even as she was saying these words, she realized they applied to *her*, too. After all, hadn't she been afraid to admit her hope-bubble mistake? Her expectation had been that she should be perfect at her job.

Moros nodded. "You're right. Beating myself up over failures or less than perfect results never helps. Especially when it comes to my art. But I still do it."

As they continued talking, time flew. Soon they were touching down in MOA's marble courtyard. "When negativity pops into your head, instead of dwelling on it, could you switch your attention to something else for a few minutes?" Elpis suggested.

"Something else," Moros repeated as they headed up the Academy's front steps. "Like standing on my head?" he asked wryly.

Elpis laughed. "Or maybe working on your art and party-planning ideas and being proud of them!"

"Shh!" Moros glanced worriedly at the other students heading up and down MOA's front steps. "Don't be so loud!"

Elpis chuckled, shaking her head at him in bemusement. "You're a good guy, Moros. And talented, too. Don't you think you could be a teensy bit more positive about your abilities and your future?"

He cocked his head at her. "Oh, but I'm *quite* positive. Positive that whatever can go wrong will," he told her with a quirk of his lips. It wasn't quite a smile, but he was getting there.

She laughed at his joke, and his eyes twinkled. He liked it when she found him funny, she realized. She wondered if anyone else at MOA appreciated his wry and gloomy sense of humor as much as she did.

"We missed fourth and fifth periods, and dinner, too," Moros informed her after glancing over his shoulder at the courtyard's sundial. Holding open one of the Academy's front doors, he waited for her to pass through ahead of him. "There's always a snacks table in the cafeteria after hours, though. Want to go eat there and work on our presentation for tomorrow?"

"I was *hoping* you'd ask," she told him as they walked down the hall. While he went to grab a table and snacks, Elpis headed to Ethics-ology to move the Pericles and Lysander figures back to Athens and Sparta on the game board. Afterward, she took the stairs to Apate's room. Apate wasn't around, so Elpis left her a note to come down and meet them to work on their presentation.

Once Elpis met Moros in the cafeteria, they continued to find lots to talk about as they snacked. There was his art, her chat with Zeus about maybe becoming the Spirit of Hope, and their presentation, of course. While Elpis outlined what their team would say, Moros finished up the drawings they'd use as visuals. Together they made a lot of headway, even though Apate never showed. Eventually, Moros remembered he had plans to practice Beastie-ball with the guys, so they parted ways. Feeling pleased with how the afternoon had gone, Elpis headed up to the girls' dorm.

"Hey! You missed fifth period," Apate greeted her as Elpis entered their room. "But who cares? Because guess what!" Apate went on excitedly. "I'm having a sleepover tonight here in our dorm room. Fun, right? Zelos and Koalemos are coming. It'll be just us four."

Elpis gaped at her in surprise. "But our Ethics-ology presentation is tomorrow. Moros and I worked out the details just now in the cafeteria. I guess you didn't see the note I left for you to join us? Since you didn't make it, I was hoping you and I could go over it together now. After all, you'll be the one doing the presenting. And shouldn't we go to bed early, so we won't be tired tomorrow?"

Pffft! With a hand on her hip, Apate made a sound of exasperation. "Don't be lame. We'll practice the presentation during lunch tomorrow. The only reason I planned this sleepover is as a welcome for you. C'mon. There'll be snacks, games, sharing secrets, doing each other's hair, and maybe dancing, too. Sound fun?" she coaxed.

Perking up, Elpis nodded. "That *does* sound fun. I've never been to a sleepover. Let's just not stay up *too* late, okay?"

"Sure," Apate replied with her usual smirk.

Elpis smiled back, still a bit *un*sure. She could hardly refuse such a rare friendly gesture from her roomie, though. Because, despite Moros's warning about Apate, Elpis still clung to the hope that this girl really wanted to be her friend. She would take her own advice and think *positive*. She'd expect the best. Not the worst!

Besides, while locked away with the trouble bubbles, she'd longed to do normal girl stuff. Like having sleepovers where friends shared secrets and did the things Apate had listed. So, yes, she was going to take a chance. What could go wrong?

Minutes later, Zelos and Koalemos arrived at Apate's room. They wore pajamas, and their arms were full of snacks, games, two bedrolls, and extra pillows.

"Let the sleepover begin!" shouted Zelos.

"Woo-hoo!" Apate and Koalemos shouted. Elpis echoed them. This was going to be fun!

Right away they all sat on beds and bedrolls to begin snacking on chips with ambrosia dip, nectar drinks, and three kinds of pie—Apate's favorite dessert, it turned out.

Elpis's gaze was drawn to a glittery ball about the size of a melon that Zelos and Koalemos had brought with them. "It's a Magic Answer Ball," Apate told her, picking it up. "My dad sells them in his store. Here, ask it a question." She handed the ball to Elpis.

"Oh!" said Elpis. She stared at the ball. "I'm not sure what to ask."

"I'll ask it for you, then." When Elpis passed the toy back to her, Apate's eyes glinted as she asked, "Magic Answer Ball, is Moros crushing on Elpis?"

"What? No!" Elpis protested, but it was too late. Apate tossed the ball in the air. It hovered in midair as she and her two friends looked up at it, eagerly awaiting its reply.

The ball spun in place a few times before speaking its magic answer: "Soon." After that, it slowly sank to rest upon Apate's open palm again.

Koalemos clapped her hands and nudged Elpis. "Did you hear that? *Soon* Moros'll be crushing on you. Wow, how dreamy!"

"*Dreamy?* Ha! He's weird. I could get a better crush—if I wanted one," Zelos claimed. Was Zelos jealous that a boy might be crushing on her? Elpis wondered. It kind of sounded that way.

"I'm not looking for a crush," Elpis insisted to the other girls. "I'm only just getting to know Moros. We're becoming friends. That's all and that's fine."

Ignoring what she'd just said, Apate exclaimed, "No problem! I can help you change how he sees you!"

Elpis let out a sigh. What part of "that's all and that's fine" didn't this girl get?

But Apate was unstoppable. "What you have to do to get a guy to notice you is to act in certain ways. For instance, boys like it when you make goo-goo eyes at them or flip your hair. You should pout a lot, giggle, and be mysterious."

"What? But that sounds so fake!" Elpis said, shaking her head doubtfully. Sure, she wanted her budding friendship with Moros to keep going, but no way was she going to do the stuff Apate suggested. It felt wrong.

"Apate's right," Zelos insisted.

Koalemos nodded, saying, "For sure."

Elpis stared at them. Obviously, she wasn't as experienced with crushes as Apate and her friends.

They'd been girls all their lives. But could what they were saying possibly be true? Surely not! She tried to change the subject. "I really hope Zeus will let me keep my girl form at the end of my week here. Becoming the Spirit of Hope would be a dream come true."

Zelos nodded, smiling. "Right. Just because there are stronger reasons for most of us—including me— to be here at MOA, that doesn't mean Zeus won't appreciate the little you can do."

Elpis's eyebrows went up in dismay. The *little* she could do? Wasn't giving hope to mortals an important enough task to allow her to claim a place (and a title!) at this school?

"She's right. I mean, think about it," Apate put in. "Athena creates useful objects. The very first week she came to MOA, she invented the olive and the ship."

"Artemis is an amazing hunter, and so is her brother, Apollo. He's a musician, too," added Zelos.

"And Persephone grows amazing pants," added Koalemos.

"Oh, I think you must mean *plants*?" Elpis corrected gently.

"Yeah, whatevs," said Koalemos, popping a chip into her mouth.

"I'm good at trickery like my dad," Apate noted.

"What am I good at?" Koalemos butted in, twirling her hair.

"Being foolish," said both of her friends.

"Oh yeah," said Koalemos, looking pleased. "I'm the Spirit of Foolishness. I sometimes forget that."

"Bet I'm better at more stuff than all three of you put together," declared Zelos.

"You're good at one-upping people, that's for sure," said Apate.

"Thanks!" said Zelos, apparently considering that a compliment. (She *was* the Spirit of Rivalry, after all!)

"Enough bragging." Apate turned to Elpis. "Back to Moros. I saw you guys fly into the courtyard after school today. I mean, if you're hanging out, seems like you must want him for your boyfriend."

Argh. On the subject of Moros, Apate was like a dog that wouldn't let go of a bone, thought Elpis. "He was just showing me how to fly in winged sandals," she explained. "And I'm trying to show *him* how to be more hopeful. He's kind of my Make Moros Smile project."

"Interesting," said Apate, munching a chip. "So Moros is just a project for you? Are you thinking that if you can help out a grumpy loser like him, you'll win points with Zeus so he'll make you the Spirit of Hope?"

Huh? Apate made it seem like Elpis was only *using* Moros to get the title and job she wanted. That wasn't true, but if she protested, Apate would probably keep going on about them crushing. Before she could think what to say, Koalemos piped up. "I've never seen that guy smile," she said. "Does he ever?"

Apate smirked. "Bet not even his crush, Elpis, could get him to smile."

"I'm sure he'll smile on his own one of these days," Elpis insisted. "And I am *not* his crush!"

"Ooh! I love bets," suggested Zelos. "What should we bet? Drachmas?"

"Pie," Apate said quickly. Licking the last crumb of pie from her snack plate, she glanced over at Elpis. "If you get the Spirit of Hope job and he doesn't smile upon hearing the news, you owe me a pie. And vice versa—if he does smile, I owe you a pie. Okay, it's a bet!"

"Really? I don't think . . . that's not exactly what I . . . ," Elpis began.

Suddenly Apate put a hand to her stomach. "Uh-oh, you guys, I'm not feeling so good," she said, flopping back onto her bed. "I think I ate too many snacks. Let's go to bed, okay?"

"Okay. Dibs!" Zelos called out, diving into the bed Elpis had slept in the past three nights and burrowing under the covers. Koalemos grumbled a bit, but then she and Elpis took the less comfortable bedrolls on the floor. Elpis didn't mind. She was too exhausted to care. Outside, the stars were starting to fade. It wouldn't be long before the sun came up. She would get whatever sleep she could before morning.

10
The Presentation

FRIDAY MORNING, AFTER FAR TOO FEW HOURS OF slumber, Elpis woke with a jolt. She sat up in her bed-roll. Looking around the dorm room, she blinked. Apate and her friends were gone! Why hadn't they woken her? And what time was it, anyway? Jumping up, she ran to the window to read the sundial in the courtyard below.

Yikes! It was already early afternoon on Friday

As she'd feared, they'd stayed up too late and she'd overslept. She practically leaped into a clean chiton and her sandals. She had just minutes to get to Ethics-ology before the start of her team's presentation!

It would be her last class, and she needed to do spectacularly well. Because it was the class Zeus expected her to excel in. After her presentation, she would go tell him about all the hope she'd spread this week, how she'd helped stop a war, and maybe even about Project Make Moros Smile. If Zeus decided she wasn't worthy of becoming the Spirit of Hope, this might be her last day at the Academy, though. The day she'd lose her girl form and go back to being a bubble forever!

Sadly, she'd missed out on spending time with

her new friends at breakfast and lunch, and during her first four classes. This was *sooo* upsetting!

Ping! As Elpis grabbed her presentation notes and zoomed down the marble staircase, the lyrebell sounded the end of fourth period. *Argh!*

As she shot through the hall, Elpis couldn't help noticing the strange looks she was getting from other students. Probably because she hadn't had time to wash her face or brush her hair! But then someone pointed at her, laughing. *Huh?*

"Have you looked in a mirror today?" a voice asked from behind her, just as Elpis was about to enter the Ethics-ology room. It was Aphrodite. For some reason she appeared alarmed.

"No. Why?" Elpis replied, shrugging.

"Come with me. Now. No arguments." To her

astonishment, Aphrodite linked arms with her, and then tugged her down the hall and into the nearest restroom. The goddessgirl motioned toward the mirror above a sink. "Look!" she commanded.

Elpis's jaw dropped as she stared in horror at her reflection. Because . . . the name *MOROS* ringed by a bunch of little hearts had been drawn on her left cheek! "They. Drew. On. My. Face?" she wailed, panicking.

"Who did?" Aphrodite demanded.

"Must've been Apate, Zelos, and Koalemos," Elpis replied. Quickly she explained that the four of them had had a sleepover in Apate's room last night.

Aphrodite shook her head in anger. "Those awful, mean girls!"

Elpis wet a cloth and rubbed at her cheek. She

whimpered when the ink didn't come off. "Moros warned me about Apate. I should have listened. Now I'll have to do my Ethics-ology presentation like this!" Unwanted tears welled in her eyes.

"Hold still. I'll magic it off," Aphrodite soothed. Quickly she chanted a magic spell:

Name and hearts, drawn in ink.
Disappear. In a blink!

Aphrodite blinked. But nothing happened. When the ink stayed put, she shook her head. "Must be some kind of permanent ink spell. Those can take days to fade. Here, let's try this." Hurriedly, she pulled a box of powder from her schoolbag and skillfully applied some to Elpis's cheek. Unfortunately, the ink bled through and was just as readable as before.

"It's makeup-resistant," Aphrodite huffed in disappointment.

Just then a memory popped into Elpis's head. "My *Opposite* Oracle-O cookie at the Immortal Marketplace! It said, 'It will be *invisible* ink,' remember? And the opposite of *invisible* ink is *visible* ink."

"So it was a warning this might happen. No way we could've figured that out, though. The final lyre-bell for fifth period will sound any minute. What do you want to do?" Aphrodite asked her. "We could go tell Zeus—"

Although she wanted to hide and cry, Elpis shook off those feelings. "No! Let's go to class. I can't let my team down. At least not Moros, anyway."

Together they rushed off to Ethics-ology. They ran into Moros as he was about to head into class. "What happened to you?" he blurted, upon seeing Elpis's face.

A single tear slipped down her cheek as they continued inside. She brushed it away as she walked, ducking her head and pulling her hair forward to cover her inked cheek. "A sleepover happened."

"With Apate," Aphrodite added.

Elpis shrugged, sure her face must be pink with embarrassment. "She and her friends drew on my face last night when I was asleep. Aphrodite tried to remove what they wrote, but—"

"—no luck," Aphrodite finished. "It's permanent ink. Well, *semi*permanent, anyway. Meant to last a few days." She glanced toward Athena, who was in the classroom, waving her over. "Sorry, but I have to go join my team. Our presentation's today too, and we're first up." Quickly she gave Elpis a hug and whispered in her ear, "You'll be fine. You got this." Then she rushed away.

"Hey, teamies," said a familiar voice.

Moros's head whipped toward Apate as she approached them in the hall. "Remove your spell on Elpis. Right. Now," he told her in an angry whisper. He was obviously trying not to draw unwanted attention.

Apate shrugged. "It was just a joke. Get over it. Wash it off," she told Elpis.

She wasn't at all sorry about what she'd done, Elpis realized. Some *friend*!

"It's *permanent* ink!" Moros growled, planting his hands on his hips.

"*Oops!* Really? My mistake," Apate said. "Unfortunately, I don't remember the exact words of the spell, so I can't reverse it." She shrugged before adding, "Sorry about that." Only she didn't sound sorry at all.

"But our presentation is today. I can't—"

"Oh, yeah . . . about that. I'm still feeling sick," said Apate, abruptly clutching a hand to her stomach.

"What? You didn't seem sick just a second ago," said Elpis.

Apate drooped her shoulders and sighed. "I told you I ate too many sweets last night. Must be from that. Anyway, I need to go lie down. You and Moros will have to do our presentation without me." And with that she turned to leave.

Elpis's eyes bugged out. "Without you?" she echoed in horror. But Apate was already halfway down the hall. She *had* looked a little green, so maybe she was telling the truth about feeling sick.

But now not only would Elpis have to face everyone during the presentation—she'd also have to help Moros give the speech! She couldn't bail. It wouldn't be fair to him.

As the two of them entered the classroom, Elpis felt about as down as she'd ever felt in her entire life. Almost as bad as when she'd been trapped in a box all those years with the nine trouble bubbles! Because there was *no hope* she wasn't about to embarrass herself right now. And, even worse, probably ruin her team's grade. (Apate might deserve a bad grade, but Moros certainly didn't!)

"What are we going to do?" she asked him.

Moros shrugged. "Give the presentation," he said calmly. As Aphrodite's group began theirs, he drew Elpis aside and pulled his colored pens out of his schoolbag. After setting them on top of a desk, he leaned close, brushed her hair off her cheeks, and lifted a pen toward her face.

She jerked her head back. "What are you doing?" she whispered.

"We're going to use your face as part of our presentation," he told her quietly. "Don't worry, unlike Apate's pens, these aren't permanent markers. I can wish these colors gone from your skin later. Now hold still. By the time I'm done, everyone'll think my drawing on you was part of our plan. Trust me, okay?"

Elpis's pale eyes searched his dark ones. He was a good guy. He wouldn't make things worse for her. Straightening, she nodded. "Okay, I trust you, *Phidias*," she teased gently.

At this, Moros's mouth twisted into an almost, but not quite, smile. He'd understood that she'd just offered him a compliment. Phidias, as everyone knew, was the skilled Greek artist who'd created a statue of Zeus so famous that it became one of the Seven Wonders of the Ancient World!

With expert strokes, Moros began to draw on her face. And then, for good measure, he speedily drew down each of her arms as well! Once he'd finished, he pulled a mirror out of his schoolbag (that thing seemed to almost magically produce anything he needed!) and handed it to her.

"Wow!" She gasped at her reflection. He'd somehow skillfully connected the existing marks on her face to become a series of clever drawings that continued down her arms. Taken together, the illustrations showed what had happened down on Earth yesterday with Pericles and Lysander. He really had made her part of their presentation!

"Team Six, you're up!" called Plato.

Elpis gasped. Luckily, she and Moros had been able (barely) to pay enough attention to Team Five's presentation to know they wanted to cast their votes in favor of Aphrodite's team's ethical choice.

But now it was Moros's and *her* turn. She couldn't let him down! So she swallowed her fear and forced herself to open her mouth and speak. "Our assigned question was this: 'What if two mighty Greek heroes from two neighboring city-states have opposing visions for how city-states should be run? Would it be ethical for them to encourage their people to wage war to make both city-states run the same way? Why or why not?'"

She let her gaze roam over the other students as she continued speaking. "As you probably know, the two city-states of Athens and Sparta are always arguing." She pointed at Moros's drawing of Athens, which covered her right palm, and his drawing of Sparta on her left palm. "We believe it's unethical to encourage war, since doing so would cause great harm to their lands, people, animals, buildings, and more." On the word "harm" she smacked her illustrated palms together to indicate a disastrous collision between the two city-states.

"If Pericles and Lysander went to war, many would suffer," Moros continued. Here he pointed to drawings of those two men—one on each of her cheeks—angrily facing off with their swords reaching and clashing across her nose. Gesturing with his hands, he flicked his fingers and made exploding noises. "Pow! Clash! Clang!"

When everyone laughed at these antics, he seemed inspired to make even more sound effects as their presentation went on, sometimes accompanied by scroll drawings he'd made on papyrus in the cafeteria yesterday. At one point, Elpis winked at the class, cocking her thumb in his direction. "This guy makes even sorta boring facts fun, right?" Lots of students clapped and grinned in agreement. Together she and Moros went on to explain all that had happened on their visit to Pericles and Lysander on Earth. And how they'd convinced the two heroes not to fight.

After a lengthy class debate in which everyone voted in agreement with Elpis and Moros's team's conclusion, Mr. Socrates handed out grades to all six teams.

"Score! Our presentation got an A plus!" Elpis shouted, gleefully punching her fist high. As she hopped around happily, Moros shook his head, eyes twinkling at her silliness. Once again, he *almost* smiled. *Soooo* close!

When all six teams' grades were posted on the board, it became apparent that theirs was the only A plus in the class. Other students praised their work, and Hades even came over and gave Moros a congratulatory fist bump. "Drawing on your team-mate was a genius idea, dude!"

Moros shrugged, but he also looked pleased as he thanked his friend. He'd magicked away the ink on Elpis's arms, but she'd asked him to leave what was on her face to disguise what Apate had done. Which was so embarrassing!

"Principal Zeus won't send you away now, right?" Moros asked, sounding a bit concerned about the possibility. "Not with our team's A plus?"

"Aw, would you miss me?" she teased.

"Maybe. A little," he said, shrugging.

Huh. Did his cheeks just turn a little pink? Elpis watched as he walked across the room and began packing up some stuff he'd left there. Just then she remembered the Magic Answer Ball from the sleepover. It had said that Moros would "soon" start to crush on her.

That can't be right, Elpis decided, shaking her head.

"Great job," said a voice. Aphrodite had come over to hug her.

"Thanks so much," said Elpis, returning her hug. "Your team's presentation was great too!"

Athena, who was on Aphrodite's team, also came over. "You guys really pulled it off," she said. "I'm happy with our team's A, but your team deserved the extra plus for creativity."

"Especially after pulling through in the *face* of a disaster," Aphrodite joked, lightly elbowing Elpis.

"Thanks to Moros's drawing skills and quick thinking," said Elpis, returning her grin. She and Aphrodite both looked over at him. He was a short distance away now, talking to one of his friends. As someone called Athena away, Elpis looked at Aphrodite. "Hey, um, can I ask you a question? I mean, you pay attention to who likes who around here. And I was wondering . . ."

"If Moros likes you? He does," said Aphrodite, nodding before Elpis could finish.

"Really?" Hearing this, Elpis felt a fluttery feeling in her stomach. It was a new feeling—one of many new feelings she'd had since becoming a girl spirit. "But Moros and I . . . we're so different," she told Aphrodite. "Oh!" All at once she recalled what this goddessgirl had said on that topic last Tuesday in the cafeteria.

"Exactly," said Aphrodite, nodding. "Like I told Apate, opposites often attract, usually because they admire qualities in each other."

"Hmm. I do admire his art skills. And that he strives to be a good person. Plus, he always tells the truth, no matter what," said Elpis. *As opposed to Apate,* she thought.

Aphrodite grinned. "Sounds like somebody's heading for crush land," she said before she went to rejoin Athena.

Was she? Before Elpis could think about this, a new voice piped up.

"So . . . looks like our team project and *your other project* were both successful." It was Apate. *Wow! She made a fast recovery!* Elpis thought.

"Huh?" asked Moros. He'd reappeared beside them without her noticing.

"Didn't you know?" Apate said slyly. "You're just a project for Elpis—Project Make Moros Smile, actually.

Last night, she bet me and my friends she could make you smile. Turns out, that's the only reason she's been hanging out with you."

Moros frowned at Elpis. "Is that true?" he asked, sounding unsure and a little hurt.

"No! I mean, maybe they thought I agreed to their bet, but I . . ." Her words got tangled as she tried to explain.

"Well, glad I could help," he said sarcastically. Then he turned on his heel and stormed off. On his way out of the room, he tossed his rolled-up sketches in the trash.

Elpis felt her stomach sink. It was the same kind of "down" feeling she'd experienced when she'd learned Apate wasn't going to help give their presentation. Was this how *hopelessness* felt? Unlike the happy, fluttery feelings of just moments ago, this felt icky. However, it wasn't her nature to stay down for long. She shook off the uncomfortable sensation, a new determination filling her along with a growing hope. A hope that—somehow, some way—she could fix things between Moros and her.

Elpis glanced toward Apate. The girl appeared positively *cheerful*. Like she was glad of the effect her words had had. Just then, a realization struck Elpis. In the same way that Moros had been *her* project, *she* had been Apate's project. But while Elpis's goal had been to *help* Moros, Apate's goal was to cause Elpis (and perhaps Moros as well) *hurt*. And this girl had succeeded! But maybe Elpis could still succeed in helping Moros?

She marched over and pulled his sketches out

of the trash. Then she glanced around, knowing exactly who she wanted to show them to. When her eyes found her target, she made a beeline for him.

Sometime afterward, Elpis headed for the cafeteria. She was about to grab a tray and join the food line when Ms. Hydra's voice blasted over the cafeteria loudspeaker. "Elpis! Please report to Zeus's office. Immediately."

Everyone in the cafeteria turned to stare at her. *Uh-oh.* Zeus must've made his decision. As much as she wanted to believe that her team's A-plus presentation would convince him to let her become the Spirit of Hope and stay at MOA, she couldn't help worrying. Because, despite the good grade, her hope bubble boo-boo *had* almost caused a war. Still, it was possible he wasn't aware of that.

Shooting a weak smile at those around her, Elpis veered away from the food line and made for the cafeteria exit. Among the many student thumbs-ups and calls of "good luck" or "it'll go fine," she also heard some quiet murmurs of "uh-oh" or "she's in trouble now."

It had been a good five days here in most ways, she reminded herself as she trudged toward Zeus's office. No matter what fate the King of the Gods had in mind for her, she'd remain hopeful. Even if the worst happened, she'd never forget the friends she'd made this week and the fun she'd had.

11

A Hopeful Spirit

MS. HYDRA WASN'T AT HER DESK WHEN ELPIS
entered the front office, so she zoomed bravely past
it and headed straight for Zeus's office. The hinge
on his door had been fixed, she noted on her way
in. However, his office was already becoming messy
again, which made her grin fondly. In some ways,
the mighty Zeus was like a little kid!

As she approached him where he sat on his throne,

her eyes widened in fear. Because there, upon a shelf behind him, sat the dreaded trouble-bubble box! Her heart dropped as she dutifully took a seat on one of the chairs before his desk.

Zeus raised an eyebrow at the ink drawings that still decorated Elpis's cheeks, but he didn't remark on them. No doubt he'd seen stranger things around here! Anyway, she was kind of glad, because she didn't want a conversation to start that would lead to Moros and the falling-out they'd just had. Well, *him* falling out with *her*, to be exact.

"I'm pooped," she huffed, nervous when Zeus didn't speak right away. "Five classes on top of my hope-bubble work will do that to a person."

"Excuse me?" Zeus's head jerked back. "Did you say *five* classes?" When Elpis nodded, he leaned forward and planted his elbows on his desktop. It was covered with what looked to be important papers. "I didn't expect you to attend *five* classes this week. Just one— Ethics-ology. I figured you'd do your hope-bubble stuff most of each day and also spend time making friends."

"Oh!" Elpis straightened, blinking at him. "I guess Ms. Hydra misunderstood. She was in a hurry my first day because the lyrebell was pinging."

"Well! It's no wonder you've made mistakes," he said, waving a meaty hand as he leaned back in his golden throne. "You were trying to do too much."

Mistakes? *Oh no!* She cringed in her chair. "So you know about . . . ? I mean, um, are you saying you're willing to overlook the almost-war between Athens and Sparta?"

"Mr. Socrates was well pleased with your presentation. And I'm pleased by the fact that your work *ultimately* prevented that war," he said, not directly answering her question.

Still, relief swept over Elpis. But then her gaze darted to the terrible box again. "Then why is *that* here?" she asked, pointing toward it. When Zeus turned to look at it, she stood from her chair, thinking to make a quick getaway if he tried to stick her back in that box.

To her surprise, his face lit up. "That? It's a gift from Hera. New hankies from her shop. In case I get the sniffles. She's so thoughtful. Need one?" He grabbed the box and held it out to her.

"A hanky? Oh. No, thanks. It looked like . . . I thought . . . um, nothing." Super glad she'd been mistaken about the box, she sank back down on her chair.

Wearing a serious expression, Zeus folded his arms across his chest and leaned back in his throne. "So, remember that mortal family in the village whose home I half destroyed with a thunderbolt?"

Elpis nodded, her interest caught.

"You blamed me unfairly," he went on. "You see, there was no perfect choice to be made in the situation."

She cocked her head. "What situation?" she asked, curious.

Zeus leaped up from his throne and began to pace back and forth behind his desk. "Their home was dangerously unstable," he informed her. "Woodworms had eaten away at its timbers. From overhead, I could see that its roof was about to fall in."

Whoa, thought Elpis. Not much escaped his notice at MOA *or* down on Earth!

"It was impossible for me to fly down and fix things in time," Zeus went on. "Plus I was in a hurry to return here to welcome Mr. Socrates and Mr. Plato to MOA. I needed to do something to make the family get out fast, before their whole roof collapsed on them."

Elpis pondered this information, then gasped. "Oh, I get it! You purposely struck the house with your bolt to *cause* that family to run outside, where they'd be safe. I'm sorry I thought you wronged them. It's just that they were so sad. Their *hopes* were dashed."

Zeus stopped pacing and flung himself back on

his throne. "I'm sure that family wished I hadn't thrown the bolt, but—"

"They were lucky you did!" Elpis exclaimed, daring to interrupt. "In fact, since the roof was about to cave in, it would have been *unethical* for you *not* to."

"Exactly!" Zeus crowed. He threw his arms wide, obviously pleased that she finally understood. "As you've no doubt learned through your Pericles-and-Lysander experience, sometimes mortals hope for things that are good for them. But they sometimes hope for things that are *not* necessarily good for them."

She nodded. It seemed all was well now. However, it wasn't clear to her if Zeus truly knew she'd been the *cause* of that almost-war between Athens and

Sparta. Not telling him seemed as bad as lying, and unethical, too.

Elpis took a big breath. "The Athens-Sparta almost-war was my fault," she blurted. "My first night at MOA, I sent out hope bubbles that motivated Pericles and Lysander in a bad direction." As Zeus listened patiently, she went on to explain how she'd accidentally led those two heroes to each think they could succeed in a war against the other. After she finished, she worriedly twisted her hands in her lap. Would Zeus decide not to make her the Spirit of Hope now?

But the King of the Gods only studied her. Speaking with wisdom, he said, "When it comes to ethical questions, there is often no single right answer. In every situation there are many considerations. Developing and using your own set of ethics can take a lifetime. Fact is, though, there *are* some choices that will always be wrong."

Elpis gulped. *Like her* choosing *to send hope bubbles to Pericles and Lysander without first determining what they were hoping for?* She braced herself for Zeus's next words, but they had nothing to do with her mistake.

"For instance, what if I went back on my word and refused to give you the title Spirit of Hope, even though you've proven you are up to the job?" Zeus said instead. His eyes were twinkling. "That would be wrong. Right?"

A zing of hopeful excitement shot through her. She scooted forward in her seat. "Yes. Wrong. Very wrong. I mean, you're right to say that would be wrong. So . . . you're giving me the Spirit of Hope job? Even though I messed up?"

He nodded regally in reply. "Yes, the job is yours. And you'll remain at MOA with the ability to switch between girl and bubble form whenever you wish."

Suddenly, happy shouts sounded behind her. Zeus's partly open office door swung wide, and a dozen students piled inside the room. "Yay!" "Woo-hoo!" "Awesome!" they called out.

Huh? Elpis jumped around to see Athena, Aphrodite, and several other students, including Pheme, who was scribbling away, recording Zeus's happy announcement on a scroll she held. No Moros, though. Still, everyone who'd come seemed as excited to hear the news about her new job as she was! They punched fists in the air and cheered. Ms. Hydra stood beyond them in the doorway, her heads (the not-cranky ones) looking pleased as well.

"Ahem!" roared Zeus, quieting everyone. "Though I'm sure Elpis appreciates your support, my meeting with her isn't over." Electric sparks flew from his fingers as he flicked them toward the crowd. "Shut my door on your way out, please. We'll be done here shortly."

Everyone shot Elpis big smiles, calling, "Congratulations!" and "Meet us at the Supernatural Market to celebrate!" on their way out.

"Well!" Zeus continued, once they'd gone. "It seems you've made friends this week at MOA in spite of your busy schedule. Good job. But back to ethics. A minute ago, you again proved your ability to make good choices, thus further earning my trust. You didn't have to tell me about the mistake you made in sending war-encouraging bubbles to Pericles and Lysander, but you did. You could have ratted out Apate for inking your face, yet you didn't."

She gasped, her fingertips rising to her cheeks. "How did you . . ."

Cocking a thumb toward his chest, Zeus said haughtily, "I'm King of the Gods and Ruler of the Heavens. I know all." But then he laughed. "Actually, Apate came to see me during fifth period today. She was hoping to get you in trouble over your team's presentation, which was happening at that very moment. She expected you and Moros to fumble without her."

"W-what did you say to her?" stammered Elpis.

"I simply asked why she'd puffed green powder on her cheeks," he continued.

"Green powder?" Elpis repeated. She'd thought Apate looked a little green as they'd talked before class, but she'd never guessed it was powder to make her look ill. What a faker!

Zeus nodded. He gestured toward the ink that still decorated Elpis's face. "She'd planned to return to Ethics-ology when it was your team's turn and 'save the presentation.' Her words, not mine. When she realized I was onto her, she admitted she was a little jealous of you and wanted you to fail, so she could step in at the last minute and appear to be a hero."

That rat! Elpis had already figured out that she'd been some kind of *project* to Apate. But until now, she hadn't recognized the full depth of Apate's deviousness—that she'd tried to ruin her chances of becoming a spirit!

"Rest assured that Apate will be punished," Zeus went on. "Still, she's the Spirit of Deceit and Trickery, so I must cut her some slack. It's not in her nature to ever mend her ways and truly be a friend."

BAM! He banged his palms on his desktop, causing Elpis to jump. "So! Congratulations on your new position here at the Academy! Now that you're a regular student, I suggest you cut back to three morning classes of your choice, leaving you with afternoons and whatever other bits of time you can find to help keep the world hopeful." He flicked his hands at her, electric sparks flying to shoo her away. "That's all! You may go now."

Dodging the sparks, Elpis practically danced her

way out of his office, stopping only when Ms. Hydra handed her a small jar. "Here, this special cream will remove all that ink," she said, gesturing toward a wall mirror. Elpis immediately headed there, and then thanked the assistant wholeheartedly as the jar's contents quickly cleared her face of markings.

"You're not the first one around here to have something like this happen," Ms. Hydra commented. "Just ask Apate's former roommates. Oh, and check in with Aphrodite tonight. I've assigned you another room in the dorm hall—one that was empty—and she'll help you get settled. You'll get a new room-mate sometime soon, I'm sure."

"Great! Thanks so much!" Elpis told her as she headed for the door. She would do her best to forgive Apate for her treachery, but she was glad she wouldn't be sharing a room with the girl anymore. Because . . . *awkward*!

To her surprise, someone was waiting for her out in the hall. "Moros?" she said. He was the last person she would've expected to see right now.

He'd been leaning against the wall, but when she appeared, he instantly straightened up. "How did it go with Zeus?" he asked. "Badly?"

Such negative thinking was *sooo* Moros that she had to laugh. Apparently he hadn't crossed paths with their other friends, who'd come here earlier to cheer for her good news.

"What's so funny?" he asked, looking confused.

Before either could say anything, Zeus bellowed from his office, "One more thing, Elpis!"

"Just a sec," she told Moros before turning from

the hallway to dart back to the outer office. As soon as he saw her, Zeus tossed a textscroll to her from his office doorway. She was so startled, she almost didn't catch it! It was pink and tied with a sparkly gold ribbon. When she spun the scroll in her hands, she saw that the words "Spirit-of-Hope Guide" were written on it in swirly letters.

"It's a one-of-a-kind guide especially for you, with rules and information you'll need going forward," Zeus informed her. "Updates and such will magically appear on it from time to time. Hera helped me create it. You'll meet her one day soon, probably at the Winter Ball." He waved a hand airily, then stepped back. "Okay, we're done. And . . . Elpis?"

"Yes?"

"Make me proud," he said.

"I will! Thank you!" she promised, clutching the scroll to her chest.

"And you!" Finally spotting Moros, who'd stepped inside the office too, Zeus pointed a finger at him. "You've been invited to design a new theater down in the Underworld to entertain the shades and keep them out of trouble. Hades asked me to ask you. Talk to him." With that, Zeus shut his office door. *Wham!*

As Moros and Elpis headed back into the hall, Moros looked bewildered. "H-how did that happen?"

"Um, you know those sketches you threw in the trash today? I might have given them to Hades," Elpis admitted. "See, one time, he mentioned that shades in the Underworld often get into trouble due to lack of entertainment. He's been trying to find a way to keep them better occupied."

When they began walking down the hall together, she went on to explain how she and Hades had come up with the idea for an Underworld theater earlier that afternoon, after Moros had left class. (Well, *stormed* out of class, actually, but she didn't *say* that!) "You've missed the deadline for the Winter Ball competition, so someone else'll be chosen for that," she said apologetically. "But I'm kind of thinking your art and design would be better suited to Hades' project. Plus, I like that you'll be doing something that'll help him with those troublesome shades. If you agree, that is."

"Huh? Of course I want to do it!" Moros gazed at her in wonder. "Wow! You—I can't believe it.

No one's ever done anything so nice for me. After the way I acted toward you and sort of blamed you, I don't deserve your help. After all, I knew what Apate was like . . . the trouble she can cause. Anyway, *thank you*."

Before she could reply, he nodded eagerly toward the scroll she held. "So you're in? A permanent student here? Officially the Spirit of Hope?"

Elpis hugged the pink scroll Zeus had given her and did a happy little twirl. "Yes!"

Watching her, his eyes lit up and he almost, *almost* smiled. "Careful there. Almost squeezed a smile out of you," she teased.

"What? You got the job?" an unhappy voice called out before Moros could reply. "Never mind. Because . . . ha! I win!" They turned to see a smug-

snacks and fun. Wrapped in a feeling of hopeful joy, Elpis returned their waves. She could hardly believe she'd be here to join in the Winter Ball celebration with them. And that she'd been accepted into this group of awesome friends!

As she and Moros headed over to join them, she smiled, thinking, *This must be what it feels like to be bumped with a "Happiness" bubble!*

Authors' Note

A note to you from Joan and Suzanne:

If you've already read our ninth Goddess Girls book, *Pandora the Curious*, you know it's a take-off on the Greek myth of Pandora's Box. In our version, GG#9, Pandora is an MOA student who accidentally lets troublemaking bubbles escape from a box. The bubbles bump other students, causing them to do silly stuff until those bubbles eventually get recaptured.

In the actual ancient Greek myth, the troubles escape from the box to forever cause problems throughout the world. Only Elpis—the spirit of hope—remains stuck inside the box. Huh? No fair!

We think Elpis should have been released too. After all, the hope in our world helps us feel better during troubled times! So in this book—*Elpis the Hopeful*—we decided to explore what might happen if Elpis *did* escape that box. We *hope* you've enjoyed this happy twist on her story!

HERE'S A // SNEAK PEEK AT
THE NEXT *Goddess Girls* SUPER SPECIAL!

Athena

"**W**OODY!" ATHENA EXCLAIMED. "SO THIS IS
where you got to!" She reached way into the far
bottom back corner of her closet and pulled out the
toy wooden horse she'd had since childhood. She'd
been searching her dorm room for it for the past
fifteen minutes!

Woody had accompanied her to Mount Olympus
Academy almost exactly one year ago. That was
when Zeus had summoned her to attend school here.
Turned out he was her dad and also the principal
of MOA as well as King of the Gods and Ruler of the
Heavens!

Now, as she sat on the edge of her bed and finger-combed the rope mane at the back of Woody's head, Athena reflected on that summons. Finding out then that Zeus was her dad, which meant that *she* was a goddess, had been quite a shock. Woody had been a source of comfort when she'd had to leave her home on Earth. It was the home she'd shared since she was little with her best mortal friend, Pallas, and Pallas's parents. She ran a hand across the four wheels attached to Woody's feet. *Whir!*

Truthfully, Athena hadn't planned to bring the toy with her to MOA, but Pallas had wisely packed him in Athena's bag. Probably realizing Woody would be a welcome reminder of her Earth home. Which he had been.

But after a year of school here at the Academy, now *it* felt like her real home. Not long ago, she'd turned thirteen. She was doing super well at school, had three best goddessgirl friends ever, and had a crush, too. In short, she was growing up! She didn't truly *need* Woody anymore. But she knew someone who might enjoy him. Her little half sister, Hebe. Hebe would be six months old tomorrow. And, at Athena's urging, her stepmother, Hera, had agreed to throw Hebe a half-year birthday party. It would be tomorrow evening, just for their family of four. It was going to be so fun!

Athena pulled back gently on the little horse's red-and-white-striped reins. "I'll miss you," she told Woody. "But if I give you to Hebe, she'll love you and play with you every day, just like I did when I was little. And I'll see you whenever I visit. Promise."

Thump! Thump! Right then there was a knock at her door. Athena cradled Woody in one arm and went to open the door. It was Artemis, one of her besties.

"Aphrodite sent me to get you," Artemis informed her. "Persephone's staying over for the weekend. They've got chips and ambrosia dip. C'mon!" Aphrodite and Persephone were Athena's other besties. Those two shared Aphrodite's room whenever Persephone slept overnight at MOA, instead of at home with her mom.

"Ooh! Chips and dip sound yummy!" said Athena. It was Friday afternoon, and classes were over. It would be another couple hours before the cafeteria served dinner, so she could really use a snack.

Noticing the toy horse nestled in Athena's arm, Artemis grinned and stepped closer to pet him. "Haven't seen Woody in a while."

Athena blushed, momentarily embarrassed to be caught holding the toy. "I'm giving him to Hebe for her half birthday tomorrow," she explained. "A half birthday for a half sister. Get it?"

"Nice," Artemis said, giving the toy horse a final pat on the head. "Hebe's going to love Woody."

A thought struck Athena. "Hey, think Aphrodite might have a cute gift box I could put him in?" Aphrodite was the goddessgirl of love and beauty. Fashion and decoration were right up her alley.

"Probably," said Artemis, shrugging. "Sounds like the kind of thing she'd have." She pushed back a lock of curly black hair back that had escaped the gold band atop her head and turned to go.

Taking Woody with her, Athena followed Artemis into the hall. If Aphrodite *did* have a box, she'd need to check that Woody fit inside it. She glanced up to see the strands of shiny silver snowflakes crisscrossing the ceiling overhead as she followed her friend down the hall. These were leftover decorations from MOA's Winter Ball in the Hall celebration, which had taken place about two weeks ago. So pretty!

"Oh, look. It's Woody!" Aphrodite exclaimed when Athena and Artemis entered her room. Her blue eyes sparkled. "Wow! Remember when he fell out of your bag and rolled across the floor in Mr. Cyclops's Hero-ology class?"

"That was on your very first day here, right?" asked Persephone.

Athena cringed a little. "Yeah. Not my favorite memory, though. The whole class laughed."

"Not the *whole* class," Aphrodite protested. "Pretty

sure *I* didn't." Her long golden hair swayed as she cocked her head. "But if I did, I'm sorry."

"No worries," Athena told her, waving a hand to brush the memory away. "That was a long time ago. And as I recall, you welcomed me to MOA from the start." She smiled at her three BFFs. "You *all* did," she added. "Which is something I'll be forever thankful for."